THE MINERVA CONSPIRACY

STONE CHALMERS
BOOK 3

RAYMUND EICH

TABLE OF CONTENTS

PROLOGUE

The Chairman of the High Council of the colony world Minerva faced the UN diplomat. The Chairman sat behind a curved conference table, flanked by the High Councillors and others.

To the UN diplomat's right, the tall, narrow windows let through and diffused a quarter of the afternoon rays from Minerva's bright yellow G1-type star. Despite the dimmed and indirect light, the diplomat's smile showed rows of gleaming teeth stark against his olive complexion. Behind and above him floated holographic lines of bullet-pointed text and a small UN logo in the lower right corner.

The hologram flickered, showed a new slide. The diplomat rested his open hand on his cocked hip. He spoke in a smooth American accent without looking at the words floating behind him.

"To summarize, when Minerva joins the Dubai Convention, multiple benefits will accrue to you. Instead of a four-month journey by warpdrive, you can instantaneously communicate with all of Earth's scientists, intellectuals, and content creators. You can export products free of tariffs—and the immense operating expenses of a warpdrive ship—to UN member states. The quick and easy travel only the wormhole can provide will give you an opportunity to recruit immigrants. Finally, you'll also receive the benefits of increased creativity when your society incorporates the vibrant diversity of the resettled."

The hologram flickered again, showed *Questions?*.

"Thank you. I'm sure you want to know more. I can stay as long as you wish to answer."

The Chairman of the High Council said nothing. He didn't need to.

To the Chairman's right, a blue-eyed man wearing a mustard-yellow blazer and a stubbly beard raised his hand. "What products does the UN forbid colonies to import to Earth?"

"Earth will accept a colossal variety of imports. Metals, fissionables, hydrocarbons, raw and processed foods, heavy machinery, consumer goods..." The diplomat made a juggling motion. "I can't list everything."

The man's blue eyes narrowed. "I didn't ask which imports are permitted. I want to know which ones are forbidden."

"Oh. *Forbidden*." The diplomat folded his arms. "Very few imports are barred by General Assembly resolutions. Weapons of mass destruction. Fission or fusion reactors. Techniques for human genetic modification. Molecular fabricators. That's all." He held his gaze on the man in the mustard-yellow blazer, then turned to the only woman in the room, a statuesque blonde with hair piled high and a Big Dipper pin high on the bodice of her crimson dress. "You had a question?"

Her voice sounded huskier than the smooth lines of her face suggested. "Under the Dubai Convention, what rights would the Minerva government have to select or reject resettled?"

"You may be assured that the resettlement authority takes the cultural background of a colony into consideration, and strives to assign resettled from a similar background when possible. Of course, the crises that create situations where resettlement is appropriate do not always conform to colonial prejudices. Though I am certain the leaders of Minerva are free of such prejudices. I'm certain your heart is large enough to welcome hungry and homeless women and children to your world." The diplomat's brown eyes softened with the final sentences. He drew in a long breath. "Anyone else?"

"No," the Chairman said. "You've given us more than enough information to make our decision."

The diplomat blinked once, but the smoothness of his next words signaled mastery of any confusion. "I'm glad my presentation has been helpful to you. Of course, should you or any member of the High Council need any additional information, message or call me any time, day or night."

"Noted."

"Very well. I'll return to the UN base camp and await word from you. If you could reach your decision in four days, I and every UN employee, both here and on Earth, would be most grateful."

"We'll make our decision by then," the Chairman said, finality in his tone.

The diplomat bowed from the waist. He turned and strode through the hologram toward double doors on the far side of the room. Against the floor of polished, blue-flecked gray granite, the hard soles of his polished black oxford shoes struck like whip cracks.

The hologram's floating UN logo morphed into a magic lamp shape, sucked up the rest of the slide, then winked out of sight.

After the double doors closed themselves soundlessly behind the departing diplomat, the Chairman and Councillors rose from the curved table. Ceiling-high doors swung open in the twelve-foot wall of ceramic tiles behind them. Strong ventilation pushed robotic miniblimps into the conference room. The miniblimps bumped the ceiling as they dangled filters to scoop up any microscopic airborne sensors the diplomat might have left.

The ventilation chilled the Chairman's face as he led the Councillors down a corridor toward the executive offices of the Minervan government. Twenty feet from the conference room, they stopped at a door to what looked like a utility closet. The bearded man in the mustard-yellow blazer poised his knuckles to knock—

The door swung open. A dozen monitors and status boards glowed in a windowless room. In the doorway stood a lean-figured woman. Her eyebrows arched and her mouth formed a coy, closed-lip smile.

"He told us exactly what you said he would," said the man in the yellow blazer. "So what do you advise?"

Her lips parted in a wider smile. She rocked her head, setting her long blond hair rippling. A gleam filled her hazel eyes.

"Surrender."

CHAPTER 1

The producer's office fit with the blue, cloud-dotted sky outside the windows. Potted plants turned waxy, deep green leaves toward yellow LED spotlights in the ceiling. Water dripped from microirrigation systems and fertilized potting soil filled the space with the rich smell of springtime.

Even better as far as Stone Chalmers was concerned, the warming weather meant girls in the streets of Manhattan wore short sheer dresses. He would get back out there soon. Just waiting for—

The producer hurried in. Tanned face and a feathered haircut. "Didn't mean to be late. My flight from Los Angeles got rerouted around thunderstorms in flyover country." He sat on an angular, black leather sofa, stretched his arm along the back, and extended legs crossed at the ankles toward Stone.

"Mr. Chalmers, Rolston—I can call you Rolston?—"

"Why not?" Stone said from a matching armchair facing the sofa.

"Rolston, glad to finally meet you. We've been trying to put together this project for, for—" The producer lifted his hand from the back of the sofa and rolled his wrist. "Tarquinia, how long has it been?"

The producer's assistant, Tarquinia, sat on the sofa six inches beyond her employer's extended hand. Plunging neckline, tight skirt hemmed above the knee, and a high heap of russet hair Stone would revel in for the five seconds he would need to loosen it. She gave Stone a look hinting she would revel in it too. "Five years ago, we acquired the rights to your great-grandfather's life story from his descendants from his second marriage. We didn't discover he had heirs from his first marriage until your—brother—?"

"Cousin."

"—until he heard about the project and threatened to sue."

The producer nodded. "We don't know what he told you, but, hand to God, from the start of this we wanted to play fair by everyone. We knew your great-grandfather had a son by his first marriage, but we had no idea your grandfather legally took his stepfather's surname after your great-grandmother remarried. Hand to God, when your grandfather's birth name disappeared from the public records, we assumed he'd died as a child during the Time of Troubles."

"Understandable."

The producer's lips clamped together. He looked away from Stone, toward the bright spring sky outside the windows. Probably subvoking to the auditory nerves of—

Tarquinia dabbed her lips with her tongue, then leaned her cleavage toward Stone. "Rolston—"

"Call me Stone."

"Stone. We know you might be unhappy about our mistake. Don't hold it against the project. Hold it against me. I'm the one who failed to dig deeply enough to ensure all your great-grandfather's heirs had the chance to buy in five years ago." She puffed out her chest. "How can I make it up to you?"

Five seconds to loosen her hair, then… an hour later he'd stroll the Upper East Side looking for his next conquest. Back on the treadmill—

Seducing women is a treadmill? What the hell has gotten into you? He forced a lazy smile. "I'll think of something."

"Glad you have no hard feelings," the producer said. "Let me tell you, we're excited as hell to bring Plutarco Blanco's story to the silver screen. It's got everything modern audiences are looking for. Romantic drama for women, action scenes for young men, and older men will love the political intrigue and the principled battle against racism."

Stone sagely nodded. "I was afraid that part might be neglected. Mestizos—you know, Mexicans who look Mexican?—envied my great-grandfather's blond hair and pale skin." He glanced sidelong at Tarquinia with a faint smirk. Her lips parted in a shocked *o*, but she leaned forward, pulled by his magnetism just the same.

Fish. Barrel.

Treadmill.

"Well, yes, right," the producer said. "We were thinking more about the racism he faced from white Americans."

"Oh." Stone drew out the word and kept his poker face.

"Our working treatment so far doesn't play up the bigotry your great-grandfather suffered from other Mexican-Americans, but script development on a project like this goes on until the last day of shooting." He shifted against the black leather. "Now, Rolston, for licensing your rights to your great-grandfather's story, we're prepared to offer you—" He emphasized the next words. "—0.05% of lifetime net revenue."

Net meaning after a thousand vaguely-worded expenses added up to a few pennies less than the gross. "0.05%?"

"Rolston, Rolston, I know that might sound low, but let me walk you through some example math here. We're expecting a budget of half a trillion dollars—United States dollars—here, but this picture could bring a trillion in domestic box office alone."

At twenty thousand dollars to see a movie in Manhattan…. "Fifty million people will go see yet another costume drama set during the Time of Troubles?"

"Easily. And that's just domestic. Latin America will easily bring in another trillion. Another half trillion for merchandising—and, hand to God, from the novelization, the graphic novel, the action figures, the other collectables, that's a conservative estimate—anyway, your share works out to a cool billion." The producer spread his hands like a car salesman. "So we've got a deal."

If Stone received a royalty check for as much as a million, he'd be astonished. But no harm agreeing. The distant cousins he hadn't seen since his father's funeral would get an ego boost from their glancing contact with Hollywood, then return to their tedious lives, longing for fortune and fame never to come.

He opened his mouth to speak. A message appeared in his vision, green letters laid over the producer's tanned face and Tarquinia's buxom curves by electromagnetic stimulation of his optic nerves by a tracery of wires around his hair follicles.

Code 909. Minerva. Report to my office before close of business tomorrow.

909 meant a special detail. Which reeked of boredom. Body-guarding some politician, likely. Minerva? A colony world so recently discovered by the UN that it didn't even have a sited wormhole mouth? And a mission so lacking in urgency Gray gave him over twenty-four hours to report?

A mission. After ten months—far longer than the inactivity period Gray had imposed at their last meeting, after his return from Trinity— after ten months, a mission.

Stone's heart beat a little faster.

"Rolston, Rolston, what's going on?"

Stone got to his feet. "An important project at work just came up."

"You mean you're leaving? I thought we had a deal here."

Tarquinia shifted her torso to give Stone a view straight down her cleavage. "I thought so too."

He kept his gaze at the level of their eyes. "Duty calls." He turned for the door.

"Rolston, Rolston, I get it." Humor with a manic edge sounded in the producer's voice. "You're playing the game. You're right, we're eager to close, but we can't give you the keys to the castle. We can go as high as 0.075% of net. Just for you. Provided you don't disclose your terms to the other heirs—"

The glass door made a faint mechanical hum as it swung toward him. "I'll be in touch," he said over his shoulder.

"Rolston!"

After an ear-popping elevator ride, Stone slipped out a revolving door from the building's lobby to the sidewalk. The noise of ten thousand cars and a hundred thousand feet reverberated off the glass and steel faces of skyscrapers. Through the press of pedestrians he glimpsed a low, faceted black shape amid dense traffic. He crossed the sidewalk to the curb. Men wearing neckties loose under unbuttoned collars angled around him. Neck-craning tourists ducked their heads and muttered "Excuse me" in cornpone Midwestern accents. Leggy young women fanned their short skirts and stared at him from wide, downturned eyes.

Imagine how much more these passersby would react if they knew how many women he'd bedded and how many men he'd killed.

His black coupe, faceted like a stealth fighter aircraft, pulled up to the curb. It popped open its door as he approached, closed it after he climbed in. In silence and cool dry air, he settled on the back seat. *UNICA HQ*, he subvoked to the car. *Priority.*

The black coupe pulled away from the curb, heading east. The message from its transponder compelled cars in front to change lanes and turned the red light at Broadway green.

North and east of Times Square, signs began to bear the logos of UN agencies and global charities. Cameras grew denser, like fungi expanding through a concrete and alloy forest.

In the mid 50s, between Lexington and the FDR, the headquarters of the United Nations Interagency Coordination Authority looked like any other eighty-story highrise. Perhaps the sidewalk in front held more anti-vehicle obstacles, concrete bollards and welded steel spikes, than some other UN buildings. The coupe turned into the garage.

Soon after, the elevator pinged at the 27th floor. The doors parted. Despite his hammering heart and churning emotions, Stone walked with forced casualness to Gray's office, rapped a jaunty pattern with his knuckles on the synthetic wood door.

"Come in."

Stone entered and shut the door.

At his standing desk, Gray looked like the upper-level bureaucrat of his job title, Assistant Director of Operational Planning. His three archaic monitors held scrolling text and a video from high altitude of dusty buildings exploding. Gray typed on a split, angled keyboard that clacked with every keypress. Not for the first time Stone wondered if the archaic input devices and displays were a cover, and Gray used the exact same transcranial magnetic stimulation hardware as everyone else.

The monitors went dark. "You're early, Stone."

And you're four months late calling me in. "I was in a meeting and needed an excuse to leave. You earned me an extra, let's see, one-fortieth of one percent of—"

"The film based on your great-grandfather Blanco's life and death?"

Stone's eyes blinked wide. How did he—?

Because he was Gray. Rivers of information from ten thousand sources flowed past his eyeballs.

"That's the one," Stone said.

"I'll buy a ticket to the premiere." Gray made a quarter-turn to his sitting-height desk and gestured at the visitor chairs facing it. "Sit, and tell me about Minerva."

Stone sat, faced a broad, glass-topped desk bare except for an inbox, an outbox, and a five-ball pendulum, all of which appeared to have never been touched. "A colony founded during the Time of Troubles. An Interstellar Transport Bureau scout ship reported the colony's discovery around the time I went to Trinity. An ITB diplomatic mission went out to bribe or blackmail the colony's leaders into acceding to the Dubai Convention." Stone subvoked up the diplomatic mission's departure date from Earth and the warpdrive flight time to and from Minerva. A date from the previous week appeared in his vision. "That mission just returned."

"And with success," Gray said, now seated across the desk from Stone. "Minerva acceded to the Dubai Convention. A wormhole is currently under construction at Hawking Station. The terrestrial end will be sited in the Mojave Desert 130 miles from Los Angeles. The ITB warpdrive ship that will tow the other end to Minerva departs Earth orbit for Hawking Station in five days. You will be on that ship."

Stone let out a long breath, and the stress of inactivity bled from his shoulders. "You suspect some ITB employees on the ship are saboteurs?"

"No."

"I get it. You want me to assassinate a Minerva politician or two."

"No."

Stone scowled. "Then what? I've been cooling my heels for almost a year and you're sending me on a mission I'm overqualified for?"

Gray peered down his nose with narrowed eyes. "You will go where I order you. Unless you wish to move your hiatus from the temporary column to the permanent?"

The pattern in the carpet caught Stone's gaze. "Of course I'll go."

"Good. Your assignment is to gather intelligence on the Minerva government relating to any threats it may pose to the UN."

Blood drained from Stone's face. Reading public websites, maybe hanging out in bars where colonial government clerks drank together and vented about their bosses. His lips clamped together and he breathed heavily through his nose.

"Minerva is unlike other colonies." The way Gray said the words made Stone frown and look up. "Every other colony we've discovered to date was founded by people looking backward from the middle of the 21st century to some imagined golden age, typically comprising ethnocultural purity or monolithic religious belief. Minerva was instead founded by American scientists and engineers who believed their golden age lay in the future. Unlike other colonies, which settled on planets with native biospheres providing breathable air, the Minervans found a waterless and lifeless rocky world and terraformed it. Their economy is heavily roboticized and computerized. They have more molecular fabricators per capita than does Earth. To the best of our knowledge, they lack artificial intelligence, and if I were a praying man I would thank God for that."

"But Minerva acceded to the Dubai Convention—"

"My hunch is Minerva acceded too easily."

Stone felt more like himself. Through a smirking mouth, he asked, "A hunch?"

"If my job didn't require hunches, a computer could do it." A pause, then Gray said, "Your cover will be an employee for a UN import regulation agency. Under this cover, you will meet Minerva government officials and corporate executives. Find whatever you can, however you can, about possible threats to the UN, and return through the wormhole after ground transportation links are established."

A grin creased Stone's face. *However you can….* How many women worked for Minerva's government and large businesses? And how many of those would open their secrets to him as readily as they would open their legs? "I'll pick up the cover story packet from Jürgen right now."

"No hurry. The shuttle from Cape Canaveral to Hammarskjöld Orbital Port launches in three days. Fly to Florida the day after tomorrow."

A mission *and* two more nights in Manhattan. This day got better by the moment. Still, work to do before he left Gray's office. "You want regular reports?"

"Yes. Copy what you find to encrypted data devices and throw them in the UN's Earthbound diplomatic pouch—you'll learn the address when you hypnogogue your cover."

"What about our field office?"

"Our field office is not yet established. The team to do so will be on your ship, under a cover which I will not share with you. Even after they establish the field office, I don't want you generating sigint that Minerva counterintelligence might pick up."

Stone's nose wrinkled. "You're worried about colonial counterintelligence?"

"No," Gray said. The tone of his next words trickled a frigid feeling down Stone's spine. "I'm worried about *Minerva* counterintelligence."

CHAPTER 2

Amid clouds of fruit-flavored nicotine vapor thick in zero-*g*, almost all of *Yassir Arafat*'s hundred-sixty passengers held onto straps and floated in front of the video walls in the ship's lounges.

On the video wall nearest to Stone, two parallel dark rings, their edges nearly touching, hung against a backdrop of thousands of stars. The closer to the rings, the more the background compressed. Crowded starlight haloed the rings' outer edges. Nanotube alloy filaments and electromagnetic grapples connected each dark ring to four space tugs. From experience, Stone read the tugs' interior schematics from their profiles. The dumpy vessels packed a life-support module smaller than a Japanese hotel room between propellant tanks and forward of a single drive nozzle in the stern.

In unison, the eight tugs fired. The dark rings drifted apart. Starlight slipped from the haloes into the growing space between the rings. Cheers and excited gasps came from the other eighteen passengers in Stone's lounge, and echoed down the curving plastic-walled corridors from adjacent lounges.

"Oh my," said a young white woman near Stone. Her pixie cut of purple hair drifted away from her face. The UN identification card clipped to her collar and naming her Merrill Mears rose and fell with rapt breaths. He'd seduced women far more gorgeous, but despite her dye job and unfeminine name, she would be in the top fifty. "It's so beautiful."

A puff of vapor smelled of rosewater and cardamom. "It would be even more gorgeous if we watched in virtual reality, alone in our room." The speaker was a swarthy male, about the same age as the woman. His soft face showed a trace of queasiness. Apparently the ship's medics underdosed his weightlessness drug. His sweatshirt hung loosely around his belly. Stone couldn't guess his ethnicity from either his skin tone or his accent—he could be from Mexico City, Marrakech, or Mumbai—but he knew the type. A man-child more at home in the interchangeable residential high-rises and international schools of the global political class than in the teeming streets of his birth city.

"In our room, just the two of us," the male repeated to purple-haired Merrill.

She turned her shoulder to him. Her rapt eyes soaked in the vista on the video wall.

A smirk touched Stone's lips. He leaned closer to the young woman. "No, you should stay here."

Her head swung around. Wide whites of eyes. Purple hair couldn't disguise black roots. "I should—" She glanced at the ID badge at Stone's collar. "—Edward?"

The man-child tried to sound tough. "Who are you to tell her what she should do?"

Stone kept his gaze on the young woman's brown eyes. "We're not on this ship alone, or even with one partner. We're on it to serve a higher purpose." He rested his free hand on her shoulder, then twisted her toward the video wall. "That."

Only one of the dark rings remained on camera. Though the ring circled the equator of the spherical wormhole, the tear in space remained invisible, except for flashing arcs along its perimeter, where gravitational lensing smeared the light of each background star into a brief, elongated blip.

"It glitters like a diamond," said the purple-haired young woman.

"I can buy you a diamond when we get back to Earth." Stone could hear the swarthy male's desperation. Which meant the young woman could too.

Stone smirked. Any time during the next four months, he could brush past the swarthy man-child at will. He slid his fingers down over her shoulder blade, then pulled them away. Merrill leaned a few millimeters back toward him.

Fish. Barrel.

Treadmill.

The four tugs pulling the wormhole drifted now, motors silent. The camera, mounted at the rotation axis of Hawking Station, zoomed out until a long, narrow ship came into view. The ship's greatest width came at two dark rings, one fore, one aft, joined by lattices and struts to the chunky modules making up the ship's elongated body. In the middle of the ship hung an empty cylinder with a diameter slightly less than the fore and aft rings.

Someone cheered. Then everyone followed suit, with the relaxing shoulders and relieved sidelong glances of people glad someone else had recognized what they saw: an exterior view of Nobel Peace Prize-class warpdrive wormhole transport *Yassir Arafat*.

Merrill stared wide-eyed at the screen. "We're going to carry the wormhole in the middle of our ship?"

"Well," the swarthy man-child said, "you know, I think so, but I'm not sure."

Her glance invited Stone into their conversation. "A wormhole inside a warpdrive cylinder? Is it safe?" she asked with a childlike tone. Subconscious or chosen, didn't matter.

Stone leaned toward her ear, deepened his voice. "Safety is over-rated, isn't it?"

Over her shoulder, wide brown eyes regarded him. "You're joking. Aren't you?"

"I only joke when I'm serious." He looked past her to the video wall. "Keep watching."

A scale popped up on the video wall. The wormhole was now about two miles from *Yassir Arafat*. White vapor jetted from the tugs' forward attitude nozzles, slowing them. Changes in the glimmering of starlight provided the only sign the nanotube alloy filaments slackened. The wormhole's equilibrator ring drew abreast of the tugs, overtook them. Lateral attitude nozzles puffed. The tugs turned over, locked their orientation relative to the ship with bursts from the attitude jets. Very precise, well-practiced by the tug pilots.

How many tedious years did the tug pilots spend in simulators?

Stone shrugged to himself. They chose their career. Every man has his place.

The wormhole drifted closer. The camera zoomed in, tighter, tighter. Red squiggles on the ship resolved into the words *UNITBS Yassir Arafat DTTV-17*. The filaments holding the wormhole equilibrator ring to the tugs grew taut.

"Now," Stone said, softly enough for only the purple-haired young woman and the swarthy male to hear.

The tugs' drive nozzles blazed with light. The wormhole slowed its approach to the transport cylinder. Teasing, agonizing, the wormhole took thirty seconds to travel the last hundred yards. Merrill and the man-child watched the wormhole's progress. Stone kept his gaze on the tugs. Short puffs from their attitude jets, all four moving in unison, imparted to the wormhole course corrections Stone couldn't see.

The wormhole's equilibrator ring slipped into the empty cylinder amidships. Moments later, the tugs' drives cut out. A faint tremor ran through the ceiling, down the strap, into Stone's hand. The purple-haired pixie caught her breath. Her male companion looked even queasier.

The image on the video wall didn't change. Only a faint distortion of the stars visible through *Yassir Arafat*'s central gap showed any sign the wormhole had actually been sited.

Passengers drifted out of the lounge by twos and threes. The swarthy male tugged on Merrill's arm four times before she said a good-bye to Stone and followed her boyfriend. Stone was the last one to watch the unchanging image. Inside the module surrounding the wormhole, techs worked, locking the equilibrator ring into its cylindrical cradle. Labor as mind-numbing as the tug pilots', but again, every man has his place.

After an hour, the camera mounted on Hawking Station zoomed

out. The entire length of *Yassir Arafat* fit on the video wall. The ship flashed multilingual warning texts across Stone's vision. Recorded voices spoke the words in all the UN's official languages. "Commencing acceleration in 5… 4… 3…."

Stone let go of the ceiling strap when the countdown reached 1. On the video wall, white-hot, wispy reaction mass poured out of the drive nozzles. The wisps thickened as the floor accelerated toward Stone's feet. He flexed his knees and an instant later landed at 0.25 *g*. He walked out of the lounge, the synthetic gravity of thrust increasing with each step. Fifteen seconds for *Yassir Arafat* to reach its standard acceleration of 1.0 *g*, equivalent to Earth's gravity. Except for a few minutes of weightlessness when the ship flipped in mid-flight for its deceleration burn, the ship would maintain 1.0 *g* for the four-month journey to Minerva.

Four months. Purple-haired Merrill crossed Stone's mind. He smiled to himself. He would keep busy.

But not simply with yet another seduction. Each night he practiced with his tool kit, shutting off the lights and pulling out spy equipment —an infrared camera disguised as a black onyx ring, a cloak of computerized fabric that wrapped infrared and UV around his body— from the canvas bag in the dark. Every morning he slipped past the elliptical steppers and recumbent stationary bikes in the gym's cardio section, and worked up a light sweat doing swings and get-ups with a ninety-pound kettlebell. He attended every thrice-weekly cultural sensitivity and diversity training session, and thus appeared to the others to be a typical white male UN employee collecting promotion points. In the sensitivity sessions, Stone struck his usual pose—aloof, sardonic, mildly flirtatious—and amplified it whenever Merrill attended. The women he flirted with responded with coy smiles, hair flips, fingers landing on his lean, solid biceps.

Merrill's interest in him rose with every sign other women desired him too.

When Stone judged she was receptive enough, he easily reeled her in, despite her half-assed resistance. "Eddie, I have a boyfriend."

"I won't tell him if you won't," he said, smirk on his lips.

Or in his cabin, still fully clothed but sitting side-by-side on the edge of the flipped-down single bed, when she said, "I really should go."

"No, stay." He put on a playfully stern look and jutted out a finger. "But you have to keep your hands to yourself."

Ten minutes later....

Fish. Barrel.

Afterward, she slunk away, blushing. Probably heading straight to her cabin to initiate sex with the man-child to soothe her guilt. She did the same after their second tryst, their third, fourth.... Each time after Merrill left his cabin, Stone shrugged. Data held in an encrypted storage device embedded in his armpit held everything Gray knew about Minerva. Might as well learn it.

Minerva. Originally, an arid planet orbiting a star hotter than Sol. After the colonists turned a hundred comets into a hydrosphere and an atmosphere, the planet's ancient impact craters acquired shallow seas, green and stinking with photosynthetic algae. Eight hundred miles south of Minerva's equator, the capital city, Euler City, straddled the banks of a freshwater river, the Strigidae, where it gouged a canyon through a crater wall and poured into the planet's largest body of salt water, the Wisdom Sea. The scout ship and the diplomatic mission both estimated Euler City's population at about eighty thousand, with another twenty thousand colonists living in smaller towns a thousand klicks or fewer from the capital. About three hundred people lived and worked at the base of a space elevator on the equator. The rest of the planet held no human life. No life at all, rather, except for mosses and fungi spread by the wind and algae seeded by the colonists from orbit.

Wait a minute. A hundred thousand colonists? In all Stone's missions, he'd never traveled to so populous a colony—and every other colony had been habitable from the moment settlers arrived from Earth during the Time of Troubles. Family sizes must be immense. A glance at the population distribution confirmed his guess. Half the colonists were under the age of eighteen standard years.

Stone frowned. He subvoked to his implantable. A map projected onto his view of his cabin's far wall zoomed out, showing all of Euler City. *Highlight schools.*

Seven red circles dotted the map.

He focused on one. *Zoom in. Visible light camera view.*

Two bright green lawns crisply lined, one for soccer, the other for ultimate flying disc. Three buildings with a cumulative footprint of about half a soccer field. The buildings' shadows showed each to have at most three stories.

This school might serve six hundred students. Nowhere near six thousand.

Maybe Minervans gave education a low priority—

—except Gray feared their high technology.

Perhaps the colonists had invented their own speedlearning technology. Squeeze a year's worth of school into a month. Not quite. Grind off the typical Earth school's busywork and ham-fisted propaganda, and you could squeeze that year down to two weeks.

The colonists might want to sell that technology to Earth.

Which is where his cover story came in. Edward Lavallette, newly-promoted to senior assistant manager in the acceded worlds division of the UN's Global Economic Cooperation Agency. Lavallette traveled to newly discovered colonies, helped business leaders navigate the mazes of red tape required to export advanced technologies to Earth, and helped Earth's superrich and superpowerful skim most of the benefit of those advanced techs. The speedlearning he'd done in his hotel on Florida's Space Coast, combined with the espionage skills grooved deep into his muscles and brain, would simplify his role as Lavallette on Minerva.

Too damn bad he couldn't end his in-flight fling with the purple-haired girl as simply. Firmly breaking it off, or simply ghosting her, could make her do something rash. Stalk him; go to ship's security with a false rape accusation; confess the affair to her boyfriend…. No. Better to carefully lower his value to her. Over the final month, he did just that. He acted needy and clingy, coldly gruff when she wanted emotional comfort, submissive to her whims when she craved his dominance.

His scheme worked. During the final week, the purple-haired girl stayed away from his cabin and rearranged her daily habits to avoid him in public spaces. Good. No distractions. Collect as much data on

Minerva as he could and ride out on the first bus through the wormhole back to Earth.

Yassir Arafat dropped out of warp sixteen million miles from Minerva, far enough to dissipate the shock wave of ionizing radiation from the warp rings above the planet's atmosphere. Twenty hours of deceleration later, the passengers gathered in the lounges. Stone found himself near a gaggle of resettlement bureau site planners and wormhole placement engineers. Menthol vape clouds chafed the lining of Stone's nose. Rumor said the first two ships' ground parties complained of allergies their entire time around Euler City. More rumor said menthol vape juice would reduce symptoms.

The purple-haired girl came into the lounge at the opposite corner. Though the others partially blocked Stone's view of her, her eyes went cold. "Gautam. I want to go somewhere else." She tugged her boyfriend by his flabby upper arm back into the corridor to the adjoining lounge.

Minerva turned a narrow crescent of its dayside to the camera feeding the video wall. On the lighted crescent, crater seas lay like green-blue discs against the lunar gray surface. South of the planet's equator, two green-blue discs overlapped like the view through binoculars in some movie. Yellow-green fringed a quarter of the shore of the largest sea and cast filaments along jagged, hairlike blue lines. Near the edge of Minerva's dark face, a tiny cluster of lights along the coast of the double sea—

Text suddenly appeared on the video wall, labeling various features. A crewman remembered to turn on the labels for the less-savvy passengers, Stone guessed. The tiny cluster of lights marked Euler City, a few minutes before dawn. More words hung over the planet's lighted limb, attached to a computer-generated white line extending from the equator. *Space elevator.* The cable and any climbing cars would be too thin to see from tens of thousands of miles. The white line ended at a dot of the same color. *Stationary orbit station.*

Lines of text in the UN's six official languages popped up in Stone's vision. A voice induced on his auditory nerves read the words. "Prepare for reduced thrust in 30 seconds. Prepare for free fall in 60 seconds. *Préparez-vous à une réduction de la poussée....*" Most of the text vanished, except for one set of the numerals. The *30* shrank and slid into the lower left corner of his vision and counted down. The *60* did likewise to the lower right.

"Where are you going to put the wormhole?" a scrawny man with a short, woolly brown beard asked a leggy woman with a long raven ponytail. Stone easily read from the man's tone, and the hangdog look of his brown eyes against his pale skin, that he longed to bed her but had no clue how.

Her sharp Scandinavian cheekbones were like a castle wall, her Korean eyes like crenelations, her plucked eyebrows, like arrows in flight. "Twenty kilometers northeast of Euler City. Off the road and rail line to the surface station of the space elevator."

"How long will it take you to prep the site?"

The Eurasian girl waggled her vape pen. "The Minervans already did it."

Eyebrows knitted like crawling caterpillars. "They did?" the scrawny man said.

She puffed deeply on her vape pen. "You think that's odd?"

The scrawny man rolled his lips in between his jaws. "I mean, I've never been out before—"

Stone turned his rolling eyes away. *No kidding.*

"—but I heard it usually takes months after the wormhole transport arrives to place the wormhole." The scrawny man scratched his bearded chin.

Vapor streamed from the Eurasian girl's nostrils. "I was told that too. We'll be ready to place the wormhole in four days."

The lower left timer reached 0. Stone's weight faded, dropping six pounds per second. He crouched and eyed the array of looped straps hanging from the ceiling.

The scrawny man frowned at him. "Hey, man, what are you doing?"

The lower right timer counted down to 1. Stone rocked his weight upward. His feet left the floor and he curled his fingers around a strap. The scrawny man and his companions flailed their arms and ricocheted off each other. Stone smirked.

The Eurasian girl flapped her arms, struggling to swim in air. She grabbed a strap near Stone and caught her breath. Voice still ragged, she asked, "You've been on a wormhole transport before?"

"No," he answered, truthfully enough. His gaze meandered down her torso and long legs, then back up to lock on her eyes. His smirk sounded in his voice. "But there are a lot of places I know my way around."

Hours before a shuttle flight to the stationary orbit station. Over a day before a climber car touched down at the bottom of the space elevator.

"Oh?" Her eyes widened for an instant.

He smirked back. Fish. Barrel.

Treadmill.

CHAPTER 3

Stone woke. His eyes shot open and his right hand reached toward the miniature plastic 9mm holstered at his ankle.

His hand stopped short as he oriented to his surroundings. He'd fallen asleep with bright sunlight outside the train windows and the tracks whispering underneath at three hundred miles per hour. He reclined in the same padded, auto-conforming seat he'd taken when he'd boarded at the space elevator; but shadow darkened the windows and the train no longer moved.

Outside the windows across the aisle to his right, a beige wall flecked with brown and yellow held a bright red e-ink sign.

Euler City

Main Station

← Ground Transportation

← Parking Garage

Somehow he'd slept through the train's deceleration into the station. Minerva's railroad engineers had great skill at slowing their bullet trains.

Or else four months of travel had dulled Stone's hair-trigger reactions.

The front and rear doors on the right side of the train car silently slid open. Currents of dry, hot air knifed through the air-conditioned car and rasped his face.

Under him, the seat moved back to upright. Stone rose, stretched his arms to the ceiling, stepped into the aisle along with the twenty other UN employees in the train car. Including—

Behind him, black hair and sharp Scandinavian cheekbones. Her Korean eyes narrowed even further than usual. The scrawny, bearded man stood behind in their row, craning his neck out the window at the sign.

Stone sniffed out a chuckle and turned his back to her.

His implanted computer pinged an incoming message notification into his hearing. Raised a red flag on a mailbox icon in the lower left corner of his vision. *From: Annika Kim.*

Who? The woman behind him. He hadn't remembered her name inside her stateroom their last night on *Yassir Arafat.*

He opened the message. Her voice burst onto his auditory nerve, louder than the shuffling feet and muttered conversations of the other UN employees.

You think you're God's gift to women, don't you, Ed? Trust me, you aren't. Jordan is ten times the man you'll ever be. I wish I'd seen that earlier on the trip here. But I see it now.

Female jealousy. What else was new? Stone kept his gaze on the door to the front of the train car. More and more hot outside air gnawed at his cheeks. *Enjoy your two kids with him in a house out in Queens.* He broke the connection.

The crowd flowed out of the train car. Stone stepped onto a platform under a curving roof made of a single sheet of some alloy. Hot, humidless air dessicated his nasal passages. He knew the term *dry heat,* but the temperature gauge projected next to the mailbox icon showed 105°F. An oven, not a sauna. A mission to Phoenix—the Arizona city, not the Dubai Convention world—would have given him the same miserable weather without an eight-month round trip. At least the surface gravity was a bit less than Earth's.

Three easy steps down the platform, a young Minervan woman in a short-sleeved sundress of pastel-yellow cotton extended her right arm toward the main station. Smooth skin, faint scents of body wash and floral perfume, blond hair held back by a plain stainless steel band the width of Stone's index finger. A Caucasian and casually dressed version of a Singapore Airlines flight attendant, the closest Earth's technology had ever come to building androids. Maybe the Minervans genetically altered her to not sweat.

Stone curled up the corners of his mouth and stared deep into her blue eyes. She met his gaze, unblinking. "Please keep moving. My colleagues will guide you to the bus to your residence."

"Will you be coming with us?" he asked with a lilt.

"No." Her blue eyes tracked back to the line of passengers exiting his train car and coming up the platform from the cars behind.

His smirk shriveled away.

The crowd carried Stone to a revolving door. He stepped in. Cold air bathed him. He inhaled deeply—the air smelled and tasted fresher than he expected from decades of experience in train stations, airports, office buildings, hotels—and tension bled from his shoulders.

A small concourse served the station's four platforms. Reflections of soft white LED lights glistened on a glossy tile floor and walls the same flecked color palette as outside. A rank of automated kiosks stood with their backs against the far wall and showed soft colors, curved edges, and antiquated icons for lockers, shoe shine, espresso drinks. Everything looked too clean, as if the station had first received passengers yesterday.

One traveller waited at a seating area near the farthest platform, sipping coffee from a mug and staring at the windows on the platform as if a computer projected data on them only he could see. He took no notice of the crowd of UN employees.

Stone made the solitary traveller instantly. He worked for Minerva's intelligence service. An amateur at spycraft: any normal person would turn his head toward over a hundred strangers from Earth.

The only other people in the station were more young women. Each wore a pastel-yellow sundress and a stainless steel hair band. Not a fashion choice, but their uniform. One waited directly in front of the revolving door and gestured the UN employees toward the center of the concourse. There, a guide with hair the same medium brown as the coffee kiosk behind her beckoned them down a corridor leading away from the platforms. Low conversations and hundreds of footsteps echoed off the corridor's high ceiling and smooth, windowless walls. At the end of the corridor, under a sign showing ↓ *Parking Garage,* a third young woman bade them descend an escalator. Another revolving door spun at the bottom, offering glimpses of a caravan of four tall, streamlined buses.

"We have to go back out in this heat?" complained Annika.

Jackson—or Jordan?—said, "I think we're underground now. It should be cooler than the train platform."

Stone went through the revolving door into the parking garage. A ceiling of gravel and larger rocks glistened with a thick coat of sealant. Underground, yes, but cooler? Maybe five degrees.

A strip of green light surrounded the open door of the lead bus. Another guide girl gestured Stone that way. Cool air from the open door wrapped him. Three quick steps up. Standard interior: a food and drink kiosk in front of him and above the nav and control computer. To his left, a center aisle ran between staggered rows of two seats on each side. A new car smell pervaded.

Stone took an aisle seat about two-thirds of the way back. Deep rows gave him enough space to cross his legs, jutting his knee toward the aisle. That should keep unwanted company away.

When his fellow passengers filled about two-thirds of the seats—fortunately, not the window next to him—the bus shifted into drive. Up a gently curving ramp, the bus emerged into dazzling daylight. The windows polarized a second later. From the sun's position in the sky, the bus headed east, toward the shore of the Wisdom Sea.

Stone turned his head. Forget orbital images and the photos snapped by the scout crew and the diplomatic mission. He would see Euler City with his own eyes.

Buildings between two and four stories, various shades of gray and white, all looking wilted by the heat. Stone soon realized why. Though essentially rectangular, the buildings' edges were rounded. The windows, all made from single panes of glass, had rounded corners. Adjoining buildings melded together in smooth curves and blended colors. Inefficient construction to build curved forms for glass and concrete—

He sucked in a breath. Concrete? He subvoked search terms to his implanted computer.

Not concrete. The dossier from the scouts and the diplomats referred to granular masses of quartz, feldspar, and mica formed and continually reformed by a framework of genetically engineered osteoblasts encoded with building blueprints. Specialized osteoblasts formed transparent regions of vitreous quartz.

Translating from tech-speak, the Minervans grew granite walls and glass windows like bones.

His gaze lowered to the street outside, dotted with aerodynamic cars whispering over blue-black fresh asphalt. Never had a street in Manhattan felt so smooth under Stone's wheels.

Stone shivered in the dense flow from the bus' air-conditioning vents.

If the Minervans grew buildings like bone, self-repairing streets should be easy.

Ahead on the left rose the tallest building he'd yet seen. Thick pillars of cream-colored granite jutted six stories upward to a broad dome. The granite pillars framed four broad, tall—murals? video displays? e-ink images?

No. Stained glass windows. Instead of a mosaic of single-color pieces of glass set in a framework, these were single panes holding regions of distinct colors. Each of the four windows showed a heroic image in an Art Deco style. Nine men in royal blue robes and three women in crimson dresses raised hands and rapt gazes toward constellations. A man in an officer's yellow dress uniform held a pistol in his right hand and a shield in his left, with a rank of similarly-equipped soldiers behind him. A man and woman faced each other, the woman handing over a green cornucopia while green 1s and 0s marched from the man's forehead, and impassive faces looked on from the background. Men in gray shirts worked at a long bench, each with a different gray antiquated tool—hammer, soldering iron, test tube, micropipettor, computer keyboard—

The bus drove on before Stone could make out more details in the stained glass. The last things he observed from the building were the words spelled by thick platinum letters jutting from the wall between the stained glass windows and three pairs of double-height entrance doors. *Center for Alignment with the Universe.*

A temple, one of about ten around the city and twenty across the inhabited part of the planet, Stone knew from reports. But to what god? The scout ship had provided no intel. The diplomatic mission had monitored traffic patterns in and out of this one. Roughly twenty cars per day trickled in and out of the parking garage. Three mornings and two nights per week, a thousand people thronged in for an hour at a time. The diplomats' informal inquiries about what happened inside the Centers met with vague answers and shifts in the conversations. Requests to attend an activity at a Center were politely rebuffed.

Stone shook his head. Months of forced idleness weakened his focus. Why care what rites the Centers practiced? Stone angled his head from side to side, working out crackles left by days of travel, loosening his thoughts in the process. The fanatics on Trinity hadn't threatened Earth with their Christian beliefs, but with their attempt to recover the last rogue warpdrive ship. Before that, the terrorists on Freeland had acted on something like a religion—the belief that people with Czech ancestry deserved their own planet—but only their missiles aimed at the wormhole mouth on their planet required Stone to act.

Religions only provided motives. Motives didn't matter. Only actions did.

"Mr. Lavallette?"

Another guide girl stood in the aisle, twin to the ones in the train station. No—a brighter yellow colored her dress, and white piping lined her sleeves and neckline. A wider band of stainless steel glowing with pinpoint green LEDs at her temples held back dusty blond hair. High enough in rank to know the UN employees' names. And attractive enough, especially after four months of seeing the same stale faces…

Stone put on a lazy smile. "How can I help you?"

She shook her head. The ends of her hair brushed the back of her neck. "My name is Abigail. I'm one of the liaison officers assigned by the Minervan government to help you and the other UN employees settle in and get what you need to work smoothly. My fellow liaison officers and I will have rooms in your hotel. One of us will be on call at all times if you require assistance. The only question you need ask is, how can I help you?"

Stone put a smolder into his blue eyes. "For starters, you can tell me when you're off duty."

Her smooth forehead crinkled. "One of my fellow liaison officers would help you then."

He raised one eyebrow and shook his head. "You know I'm not talking about your professional duties, don't you?"

Abigail's voice grew cool. "Of course I do, Mr. Lavallette. It appears I must tell you that fraternizing with you is strictly forbidden."

With a slow lilt he said, "I'm sure that's what your handbook says—"

"I'm an unmarried young lady with a reputation to uphold."

Damn, she played aloof. Ah, the chase was half the fun. Stone's smirk widened. "I have a reputation of my own. Which includes never kissing and telling."

Abigail folded her arms over her chest. "We're nearing the hotel and I have more introductions to make. Good day, Mr. Lavallette." She stepped past him. Thin cotton rustled over her smooth pale legs. She didn't look back.

Losing your skill at the game? floated through his mind. From the Lavallette persona?

No. From himself.

Stone rubbed his eyes. Losing his skill? Couldn't be happening. Anywhere in the settled galaxy, women remained manipulable creatures. He would win the game. At most, playing it on Minerva might require different tactics.

Then into view on his left came something that put skirt-chasing toward the back of his mind. Two- and three-story buildings of stark white and classical styling rose from the middle of broad green lawns. Steel fences stood between the lawns and the sidewalks. Minervan government buildings, aping the style of United States government facilities in Washington. The Minervans were Americans, after all, and doubtlessly shared with most American-settled colonies a nostalgia for some well-governed golden age. Right down to the apparent lack of security. The cameras presumably hidden in the fencing wouldn't stop a truck bomb, let alone a thousand rioters or a squad of trained commandos.

A closer look beyond the little capitols and supreme courts revealed a pale blue wedge nearly invisible against the cloudless teal sky. Wait. Was that precise shade—?

His implanted computer copied sensory inputs from his optic nerve. His implant effortlessly performed an RGB analysis and mapped the location at the same time.

The results appeared in his vision as a glowing outline of the wedge with accompanying text. Stone read, then laughed.

Not pale blue. *United Nations* blue colored a thousand-foot skyscraper holding enough hotel rooms, recreation facilities, and office space for ten thousand UN employees. A skyscraper built sometime in the last eight months and towering over every other building on the planet. Towering over government facilities and Centers for Alignment with the Universe.

Maybe the Minervans could grow skyscrapers in hours, but they knew to bend the knee and build them for the UN.

Stone smiled and lolled his head back. He closed his eyes, able to relax. Gray worried about nothing.

CHAPTER 4

T he elevator slowed, lifting Stone's stomach back where it belonged. He swallowed to clear his ears as the doors opened on the one-hundredth floor.

Cocktail party chatter mingled with a muted trumpet soloing over piano and upright bass. Behind the short near side of the long, narrow triangular bar, robotic arms clattered ice inside shakers. Stone spoke three words to a parabolic microphone and ten seconds later a robotic arm lowered a glass of seltzer with a lime wedge in front of him.

He sipped. He'd been productive during his first full day on Minerva, despite fitful sleep from a stuffy nose and a mild headache dogging him most of the morning. Productive, and now time to play his favorite game.

Drink in hand, Stone sauntered to the right through a crowded mass of UN employees. Unlike his gray slacks and royal blue oxford shirt, the others dressed wildly, checked patterns, billowing sleeves, upturned starched collars. The trend for twentysomethings the week before *Yassir Arafat* left Hawking Station, now three months out of date on Earth. Many of the young UN employees were already drunk, and most others were well on their way.

A spicy vape, cumin and turmeric, wafted in Stone's face. "My maaaaan." Sweat plastered a pudgy fellow's black hair to his olive skin. Brown eyes looked down at Stone's drink, went wide. "Vodka tooooonic!"

Stone's nose wrinkled. "Sure." He slapped the man hard on the shoulder and pushed him aside.

Keep moving. Stone cut through the crowd. Rounded the corner of the bar. The riot of different checked shirts would bring back his headache before long. Where were the Minervans?

He pushed into an open area. The corners of his mouth lifted. Minervans in clusters of four to six, women in black dresses and diamond necklaces, gray-suited men with hair pomaded down and solid-colored ties knotted up. Only on a colony world could everyone in so stylish a crowd be white. The Minervans stood far from the bar, close to the glass wall lining this long side of the wedge-shaped hotel's penthouse.

Distance from the bar explained only a little why the UN employees didn't mingle with the Minervans. A glance down explained the rest. This uppermost level jutted outward from the main structure of the hotel. The glass walls behind the Minervans curved at the bottom to join the floor. While the UN employees kept their footing on the glossy granite near the elevators, the Minervans seemed to levitate in empty space.

Among the Minervans, Stone found a familiar face. Gaze straight ahead, he strode onto the glass floor toward a group of five. He extended his hand toward a man with a narrow, bulbous nose. "Mr. Ranta!" As part of the Lavallette persona's duties, Stone had visited Ranta's office four hours before.

They shook hands. Stone stamped the heel of his black wingtips against the transparent floor. "Is this one of yours?"

"I wish. My company can't grow glass both as thick and transparent as this floor. Not yet."

"If you can be the first to break in to the Earth market, you'll make huge profits you can plow into R&D." His gaze shifted a fraction, toward a dazzle of diamond on the upper slope of a woman's breast.

Ranta's eyes narrowed for a moment. "Let me introduce you to everyone."

The other man in the group, Yeardley, manufactured equipment for growing organs from a patient's stem cells. His equipment worked well for livers. "Looks like your colleagues might need it."

"All I can say in their defense is that they spent four months cooped up on a ship as spacious as two floors of this hotel."

Yeardley's wife angled her head to Stone. "So did you, but you haven't drunk yourself sloppy tonight."

Bleak memories of his dead alcoholic father stirred. Stone stifled the memories. Shrugged. A smirk touched his mouth. "I kept myself busy with—" He gazed into her wide brown eyes. "—Pursuits."

She quickly looked away, then leaned against her husband and wound her necklace chain in her fingers. Yeardley scowled. Ranta shuffled his feet forward, partially eclipsing his wife from Stone's view.

The fifth member of the party spoke in a husky yet alluring voice. "And what pursuits would those be, Mr. Lavallette?"

The woman stood nearly as tall as Stone. Blond hair billowed around her face. Crow's feet wrinkled the skin at the corners of her eyes. A long, crimson dress clung to her trim curves from collarbone to mid-calf. High on the left side of her chest, jewels woven into the velvet glittered in an image of a half-familiar constellation.

Identify, he subvoked to his implant.

Text popped into his vision. Diamonds as the Big Dipper and Polaris, the north star, in line above the Dipper's leading edge. His implant labeled a round yellow tiger's eye low to the left as *Unidentified.*

Stone returned his gaze to her blue eyes. She regarded him and the corners of her mouth curled up ever so slightly.

If he'd met her at a cocktail party in Manhattan, he'd consider attempting to seduce her. She might possess enough mature sultriness to make up for the faded bloom of her beauty. But here on Minerva, where single women fretted about their virtue and married men guarded their wives, he had no better prospects.

Plus there'd be an extra thrill at seducing a woman of her vocation....

"My pursuits on *Yassir Arafat*?" Stone put on a lazy grin while keeping eye contact. "I'm afraid they lacked any spiritual uplift—Reverend?"

"Facilitatrix. Sheila van Bentum." She extended her hand.

He bowed and kissed it. His lips felt the faint pliable ridges of veins on the back of her hand. The crisp floral scent of her perfume lifted his eyebrows. He straightened his back and slowly pulled his hand away. His fingers slid over smooth skin.

"Fa-cil-i-ta-trix," he said. "Not Reverend? The Centers don't provide guidance in spiritual matters?"

"Not in the manner of a church or temple on Earth. You see, Mr. Lavallette, when one lives in alignment with the universe, all one's actions are equally spiritual. And profane."

"An intriguing perspective. And please call me Edward."

"Edward." She tasted the name.

Time to neg her a little. "Just how much can you know about religion on Earth?"

Her eyes blazed like sapphires. "I was born there."

Stone's jaw fell. "Born? You… you tell a good joke." He glanced to either side. Ranta and Yeardley's faces showed no humor.

"I'm ninety-seven," Sheila said.

Stone regained his poise. He gave a lazy smile. "You don't look a day over seventy."

Angled head, arched eyebrow. She looked like a fit fifty-year-old from the era before longevity tech, and she knew he knew that.

Longevity tech. More advanced than Earth's. The Lavallette persona darted around his subconscious, wanting to make calls, schedule meetings, bring that tech home—

Tomorrow. As for tonight… did he still want to seduce a woman nearly three times his age?

Oh yes.

Stone touched her elbow. "I'm curious how a young woman on Earth became a priestess of a colony world's state religion." He applied gentle pressure in the direction of the window wall.

"I would love to tell you my story. But I don't want to bore these well-aligned people." She murmured good-byes to the Rantas and the Yeardleys, then stepped backward on thick black heels.

A few seconds later, Stone squeezed her elbow through the velvet sleeve, stopping her feet six inches from where the floor curled up to the wall. In the window, the lights of Euler City glowed through the party's blue-white reflections. Three hundred yards below their feet, the waves of the Wisdom Sea spumed up the crater wall.

"The twenty-first century was an era of social upheaval," Sheila said. "In all such eras, the traditional beliefs and rituals that assure us —all levels of *us*, species, society, and individuals—of our place in the universe shrivel. Many perish completely. But our need to know our place in the universe remains, like a seed craving a patch of dirt and a trickle of water."

"Poetic," Stone said.

"During my college years, that need was in me. But the dominant culture only wanted young people to seek meaning by…." Her gaze knifed past Stone. Slashed across the drunken and horny faces he'd pushed through to get here. Her face showed the tracks of dark thoughts behind it.

"The profane only, without the spiritual."

"Exactly." Sheila smiled. "I lacked alignment with the universe and would have been miserable the rest of my life without knowing why. Then I met the First Facilitator."

"How?"

"He lived and worked in a warehouse in a neighborhood of the city still half in ruins from the street battles between Chicanos and Bantu-Americans in the '30s and '40s. He was a theoretician who knew what a future where everyone lived in alignment with the universe would look like, and wise enough to know that many practical and detail-oriented people would have to get their hands dirty to build that future."

A cult leader. Probably surrounded himself with young women with daddy issues. "You were one of those people?"

"I had a few of the needed skills. Enough to take my place on the team. The First Facilitator provided some money and equipment to start us on the work. Doing the work brought me toward alignment with the universe for the first time in my life."

Stone trailed the backs of his fingers down her right arm. "How did you come to Minerva?"

She brushed a blond strand behind her ear. "Zachary Euler had graduated many years earlier from my university. Many of my team members were my classmates, graduate students, or had recently finished their degrees there too. Euler heard of our work through the alumni network and came to visit. He had profited handsomely during the Crisis of the Twenty-First Century, but still he craved an alignment with the universe that his trillions could not buy.

"After two days talking with the First Facilitator," Sheila added, "Euler took up our cause."

"A trillion here, a trillion there, and soon you're talking real money."

"Euler opened his checkbook, yes, but he did much more. He publicized us. His name alone gave us credibility. And despite his prominence, Euler deferred to the First Facilitator on everything. With one exception."

"Stay on Earth," Stone said, "or colonize a distant planet."

"You have it. Euler commissioned an exploration ship months before he met the First Facilitator. He said in hindsight it was a fumbling attempt to align himself with the universe. Then the ship returned to the solar system and reported finding a world meeting Euler's criteria." She spread her arm to indicate the night-dark portion of Minerva visible from the window.

"The First Facilitator wanted to stay on Earth," she said. "The team could focus on the work, instead of putting most effort into constructing a biosphere. The team could recruit more people and would have access to more infrastructure, and could achieve the final stage faster. The main reason he wanted to stay, though—I grasped it right away—was because he wanted to bring everyone on Earth into alignment with the universe. If he could do that, all Earth's problems would be solved, and there would be no need to flee."

Solve all Earth's problems. Sure, any millennium now.

"How did Euler win the debate?" Stone asked.

Her tone of voice shifted, clashing with cool jazz trumpet. "US government agents raided, arrested the First Facilitator and several team leaders, and confiscated much of our equipment. Almost everyone sided with Euler after that."

Except for the few who realized Euler had pulled strings to get US agents to eliminate his rival for control of the cult. "Then you came here."

"I was on the first of three ships. We worked hard those next years, some of us sending comets to graze the planet while others perfected the techniques of alignment with the universe. We survived a second great loss when Euler died on Earth recruiting a fourth shipful of colonists. But we persevered. We built a habitable world and gave purpose in life to all its inhabitants. And I am humbled to have played and continue to play my small role in our adventure."

Sheila didn't look humble. Quiet pride filled her mature features and her sapphire eyes. She leaned closer.

Time to close. "Your life has been an intricate tapestry," Stone said. "Let's add a new thread to it. Twenty floors down. My room."

Her features remained open, yet: "No."

Stone flicked his gaze down and up her torso. "Your mouth says one thing, but the rest of you—"

"Not your place. Mine."

UN employees could leave the hotel at any time in a car checked out from the motor pool. A Minervan counterintelligence officer would trail him, would gather evidence of his tryst with her, but that would be Sheila's problem. "Sure. I haven't been inside a Minervan house."

She moved her mouth close. Her breath smelled of one vodka drink. Her husky whisper filled his ear. "You were so curious about alignment with the universe, I thought you might like to see a Center from the inside."

His interest immediately rose. "Talk about the sacred and profane."

Eyes suddenly tight, Sheila glanced about. Her facial expression eased but a hunch in her shoulders revealed unease.

"Send me the address," he murmured. "You leave first. I'll take a different elevator to the garage and ride in my own car. No one will see us leave together. I know how important her reputation is to a lady of Minerva."

She smiled wryly. "You have no idea."

CHAPTER 5

His borrowed blue coupe rolled to a stop under a granite buttress as stout and curved as a rib of leviathan. The coupe popped its door. Blue-white light washed over the space under the buttress. A spotlight shone on dappled steps leading up to an automated sliding door. A sign above the door read *Enter, and Know Yourself.*

Stone climbed out of the coupe, a smirk on his lips. Know himself? His interest lay in knowing Sheila van Bentum. In the biblical sense.

The coupe shut its door and drove into the main part of the subterranean parking garage to wait for him.

He took the steps. The sliding door opened. Cool air cloaked him as he entered.

At the head of a broad spiral staircase, he came to a long hallway. Signs pointed left and right to meditation rooms. Straight ahead, down a short passage, waited the auditorium. And Sheila.

Stone strode vigorously forward. Another door slid out of his way.

He entered a cavernous space. Dim accent lights glowed where sandstone-colored walls met a floor of a slightly darker shade. From the street outside to his left, the lights of downtown Euler City cast swatches of gray, green, yellow, blue, and red across the upper portions of the walls and the lower reaches of the vaulted ceiling. High on the deep indigo vault, a familiar pattern of lights twinkled like bright stars. He'd entered the auditorium from the east. The Big Dipper's leading edge pointed to Polaris at his right. Which meant the bright yellow disc low in the vaulted ceiling opposite him represented Venus as the evening star.

"Welcome," Sheila said. She stood ahead to his right, in a center aisle between ranks of oaken pews. She came toward where the pew nearest him would lead him to the aisle. Thick carpet muffled the falls of her black heels.

He went to the aisle, glancing at the pew backs to his right. Dense hardbacks showed titles *The Way of Virtue and Other Books* and *Music Aligned with the Universe.* His fingertips brushed along tight-packed pages, jumped up to a smooth oak beam atop the pew backs. Jumped to Sheila's elbow.

Enough light filled the vaulted room to show the sapphire-blue in her eyes. "For a non-religion, you've got a regular cathedral." He flexed his eyebrows upward. "Vaulted ceiling, stained glass windows...."

"The First Facilitator studied psychology and comparative religion in college," Sheila said. "Even though he knew establishing true alignment would require scientific insight and technical skill, he also knew that symbolism and group ritual would help people accept their place in the universe." She broke eye contact.

Stone squinted at the ceiling. "Sure, but why Earthly constellations? Polaris almost certainly isn't your north star—south star from this hemisphere—and if you could even see the stars of the Big Dipper, this far from Earth they'd draw a totally different picture." He nodded toward the evening star on the far side of the auditorium. "And Venus?"

"The astronomical symbols reflect our origins on Earth, in the northern hemisphere, in Western civilization. They also provide metaphors for alignment with the universe: Polaris, a lodestar; the Big Dipper, a vessel for the bounty of the universe; the evening star, a sentinel that observed our labors in the day just finished and lights our rest in the evening just begun."

There would be some alignment between the two of them this evening, but hopefully not too restful. Stone brushed his upper arm against hers, then turned his head toward the stained glass. "You also use colors as metaphors."

She shifted her weight against him. "Colors have borne symbolic weight since before the dawn of Western civilization. Blue evokes logic, objectivity, constancy, and dispassion; red evokes passion, subjectivity, lability, and partisanship."

The headlights of a passing car sent a wave of brightness across the male and female clerics raising their hands to the heavens. "Blue is masculine, red is feminine?"

"Close. Blue represents masculine energy, red, feminine. Both energies are at work in each person at all times, though the proportions differ from person to person and time to time."

Stone cupped her ear. Ran his fingers through her blond locks toward the back of her head. "Your feminine energies are running strong right now." He pressed his fingers together, grasping strands of hair, and faintly tugged.

"Much as masculine energy runs through you." She moved her head forward and he released his grip. "Come with me."

Sheila turned away from the stained glass and walked toward the front of the auditorium. The carpeted aisle ended at a dozen ivory-white steps as wide as the space. The steps ran up to a dais. Lectern to the left, an altar of white granite at the center. Behind the dais rose blank walls, e-ink displays, he guessed, with a choir loft above them.

He sped his pace, caught up with her. Put his arm around her waist. She leaned against him.

At the foot of the steps, she pulled to the left. He followed, puzzled for a moment, until he saw why. Thin seams in the ivory-white steps marked a rectangle as wide as the altar and as high as the stairs. Another seam down the middle divided the rectangle in half.

A retractable, not-so-hidden doorway.

What secrets lay within?

Sheila led him up the steps to the left of the retractable doorway, and across the dais between the altar and the lectern. The back wall held a plain door, not even with a knob. The door swung open soundlessly as they approached, revealing a hallway running straight away before bending to the right.

After passing a meditation room and offices with hers and other facilitators' names embossed on closed doors, they entered a study. Ceiling lights came on automatically. Nailhead trim decorated brown leather armchairs. Ten chairs surrounded an oak conference table with scenes from the stained glass windows carved in the wide upper portions of the legs. Gray would approve the decor.

Sheila gestured to a loveseat matching the armchairs, far from the room's curtained windows, then went to a cabinet nearly her height. The cabinet opened its doors. Interior lighting glinted on glasses, bottles, a steel sink and faucet. "What will you drink, Edward?"

His forearm on the arm of the loveseat, Stone said, "Sparkling water with a citrus wedge, if you have it."

Bottles thunked and thudded as she rummaged inside the cabinet. "We do."

Carbonation hissed into a glass. A machine hummed. Ice clattered. Sheila pulled a cork with a *thwoom*, cracked open a twist cap, and poured twice.

Stone guessed her state of mind from experience. A stranger, a one-night stand, second thoughts. And liquid courage to numb her fears.

She settled next to him on the loveseat. He took a highball of sparkling water from her, raised it, and drank.

He winced. Bitter with minerals and too much sour lemon.

"Not what you're used to?" she asked.

"Nothing on Minerva has been, so far." He fortified himself against the taste of the sparkling water and drank deeply.

"Good," she said. She sipped a pallid red drink, then fixed her blue eyes on his. "I would hate to think you've ever met a woman like me."

Stone extended his arm along the back of the loveseat, behind her. "A non-priestess of a non-religion? Who's three times my age? Never had the pleasure, till now."

Sheila arched her eyebrow. "You mean two and a half."

"Let's not quibble." He poured the rest of his sparkling water down his throat, set the empty glass on a side table.

"My age doesn't bother you?"

"No. Does it bother you?"

"Prove it doesn't bother you," she said. "Kiss me."

Normally he would have strung the tension out longer, but when she put it like that, time to seize the moment. He leaned forward. Her lips pressed full and soft against his. The tart taste of cranberry juice, the aseptic scent of vodka. Her sapphire blue eyes remained open, peering at him.

He took her gaze as an invitation. Lifted his hand to cup her breast. His hand felt too heavy to move.

Sheila moved her head away from him. "Sit back."

She wanted to be the assertive one at first. Fine by him. He would pay her back with interest.

Later. He sat back, hands on his thighs, a lazy smile on his face.

"Empty your pockets onto the side table."

His hands moved to his hips before he could think about complying. "I don't carry erectile dysfunction tablets because I don't need them."

Sheila's eyes looked cooler all of a sudden. She said nothing. His right hand pulled out a pocket computer, backup to his implant. His left retrieved a flat, supple stick as long as his little finger. An encrypted memory stick. He had more in his hotel room. The memory stick's transparent, antistatic wrapping crinkled in his fingers.

He watched his hands set the three objects on the table as if he watched an actor on a video screen. A frown furrowed between his eyes. The hell?

"Send no messages and acknowledge the receipt of no messages through any computer. Stop any recording of audio or video data to any computer. Delete any stored audio or video data you recorded after you arrived at the party from any computer."

"What's going on?"

She rose and took two long steps away from him. "Stand. Walk to the conference table with your arms at your sides. Put your hands on the table, move your feet wider than shoulder width. Stare at the table between your hands. Do not move."

His body lifted itself from the loveseat. Walked to the table. Stopped at one of the short sides, between carved priests and a shield-bearing soldier. Set down his hands and shuffled his feet as she'd ordered. His mind had no choice but to go along.

"You dissolved a drug in my drink." She'd left him enough free will to speak.

"Thirty seconds to figure that out? I expected better." Sheila crossed the room. Her hands patted down his shoulders, arms, pits. An amateur's hands, knowing the theory of how to frisk but lacking practice. He might have a chance.

His hands felt bolted to the tabletop. "You didn't have to. I'm man enough to act out any woman's kink."

Velvet rustled. Her hands ran down his legs. Stopped at his right ankle. Pulled the compact 9mm from its holster. A second later, plastic clattered on leather.

She knew he was more than a UN bureaucrat. How?

His heart slammed inside his immobile chest. Not how.

From whom?

She untucked his shirt and reached inside his waistband with hands as cold and clinical as a nurse's. Then she stepped back. "Hands to your sides."

His hands swung like sides of beef on a slaughterhouse's hooks.

"Turn around."

He did. The crimson velvet of her dress contrasted with the blue ice of her eyes.

"Walk at a medium pace out the door. I will direct you where to go after that."

Stone's body moved moderately. His insides writhed like trees lashed by storm winds. He managed a deep and calming breath.

Keep your mind clear and you might walk out of this. The drug would wear off eventually. Don't eat or drink anything she offers.

The door opened. He went through and paused in the hallway. She followed. Gave instructions. Left. Another left. Through a door under an exit sign. Stone's mouth dried. A stairwell down. To the parking garage or the outside of the building, either way, a chance to escape....

At the next landing, the stairwell continued downward into shadow. "Through this door."

Still inside the Center. Why? A non-religion wouldn't perform human sacrifices. Right? And she wouldn't want to spill blood on the beige carpets or the crinkly pages of secular scriptures.

His thoughts raced while his body plodded at her command further into this level. His internal compass still worked, she ordered him somewhere under the dais. Not far from—

To his left, the floor of a short hallway ramped up and curled to the right.

Stone rounded the corner. Light spilled from an open door. Machinery hummed inside.

"Enter."

A trusswork of metal shelving and sliding racks filled the back and side walls with a squared-off horseshoe of computers, e-ink displays, and other equipment. Some appliances reminded him of hardware in the genomics lab at UNICA headquarters, but most he couldn't identify. Generic boxes of off-white plastic, green LEDs, cooling fans. Conditioned air spilled from a vent. Stone tucked his arms against his sides.

In the center of the horseshoe, a chair swivel-mounted to the floor showed its back.

"Sit," Sheila said.

His body moved. He noticed black vinyl covered a padded seat, back, and armrests. Hope surged for a moment, no straps.... but with the drug, she didn't need straps. He sat, just as some nameless drudge from the outer boroughs might in a barber's chair near a train station, or a chair in a dentist's office in Queens.

Except a dentist's office would have a light mounted on a pivoting arm from the ceiling. Not a hemispherical helmet, descending with a whir.

He jerked his head around. The helmet paused.

"Sit up straight with your arms and head still."

Stone's body did as she ordered. The helmet descended the rest of the way. Folded over the tops of his ears, let them flick back up. A soft inner lining snuggled his head. Two e-ink displays formed a sterograph.

Alignment with the Universe.

Initial consecration. Adult subject.

A thud of binaural beats ping-ponged from ear to ear.

"What are you doing?" Stone asked.

"In this place, in this moment, we work together, to all high emprise consecrated." Despite the helmet's padding and the binaural beats, Sheila's words came to him, clear and solemn. A priestess intoning a phrase from ritual.

"Edward Lavallette. The time has come for you and us to find out who you truly are."

CHAPTER 6

Edward Lavallette? She hadn't pierced his cover….

In 3d appeared an inverted L assembled from cubes, most white, two black. Two white cubes held black circles in their faces closest to him. The inverted L slowly rotated. A different white cube showed a black circle, and one of the black cubes, a white one. Rotation showed another slightly varied pattern on the third face, the fourth.

Duplication. The second inverted L differed slightly, more contrasting circles on one side, fewer on another. More rotation. Another duplication. More variation, but the pattern—

An IQ test of visuospatial reasoning. A set of four more inverted Ls popped up, one of which would complete the pattern of variation.

That's all this was? Why lure him, why drug him?

Piss on her. He looked away. The stereograph inside the helmet followed his gaze. He shut his eyes. The four possible answers remained in his vision. Of course the third was correct, but he wouldn't give her any satisfac—

A prick in his right ring finger. His arm tried to lift off the chair but Sheila's command locked his arm in place.

Pairs of words shot by. *Activate Actuate. Consign Condign. Instigate*

Investigate. Don't play her game—his mind darted over the meanings anyway. The next pair appeared before the definitions fully formed in his mind.

The hell kind of IQ test was this?

Verbal analogies followed. Algebra and geometry problems. Like his senior year of high school, taking the college aptitude tests—

Green paint peeling off concrete block walls. Cops at their desks outside the holding cell, sipping oily-smelling coffee from white foam cups, glancing through the bars. Through him.

Adolescent indignation burned Stone's eyes. You can't do this to me! My parents come from families you've heard of! You'll write parking tickets in the Bronx if you don't let me go!

Later, unease nibbled at him. The girl—Melanie? Melody?—lied. The sex had been consensual.

Consensual enough. They'd both been drinking at the hall party in the dorm. But just because her inhibitions were down didn't make it rape.

Hours in the cell. A hole expanded inside his gut. Mom cavorted with her latest boyfriend on a Mediterranean beach. She wouldn't come. Dad? The hole's crumbling edges exuded bitters. Too drunk in his study to answer a call.

—*Christ damn it how does Sheila know this?*

Out of Stone's sight, a door creaked. Measured footfalls.

A cop looked over the thick rim of his cup. Freckles surrounded a once-broken nose. "Whaddaya want?"

A brisk and formal voice. "Your prisoner."

Stone didn't know the owner of the voice. But the diction, the tone. Maybe Mom from six timezones away had called—

"You frat boy's lawyer?"

"No."

The cop scowled. "If you ain't his lawyer, boyo—"

A faint snick of an attaché case unsnapping itself. The rustle of heavy paper.

The cop leaned forward, squinting. Then he jerked his head back. "Hey, why din't ya tell me?" He rose so fast his chair spun its cracked vinyl arms. He waddled to the cell door, fumbling with keys on a handheld computer.

Stone stood up. He wanted to reach for the bars, but resisted the urge. He wouldn't show weakness in front of some cop. If not his lawyer, who came to rescue him?

More measured footfalls brought the owner of the brisk voice into view. Two piece suit, complete with a diagonally-striped tie impeccably knotted at a fully buttoned collar. Wavy hair, brown going gray; high forehead; and a pair of piercing gray eyes.

In an instant, the hole in his gut vanished. Filled with warm jitters.

In an instant, Stone knew his destiny had changed.

The memory froze. Rewound the cop back to his battered swivel chair, Gray back out of Stone's life. The hole reopened in Stone's gut. Its jagged edges burned with bile.

Sight, sound, smell, mood swirled, reformed. The scent of carpet shampoo wafted up from the maroon carpet under his stomping feet. A familiar painting, Model T cars clogging Times Square two centuries ago, its oil paints textured with brushstrokes, near the apartment door. The reddish-brown door, trim and proper like the rest of the hallway, hiding the shambling mess inside.

Sheila couldn't know this. The helmet and all the computers around the room tapped his memories.

Stone shoved his thumb against the doorknob's reader. The goddam biometrics better work or he'd stand in the hallway for hours.

The door snapped back its latchbolt. Stone pushed harder than he meant. Not really. Stone stepped through and the door bounced off the coiled-spring doorstop. He slammed the door shut behind him and stalked toward the study.

Dad sat at his workstation. A spiraling screensaver gyred over the angled touchscreen. The old man—

How old was he when I graduated? Fifty-five? Christ he looked like hell.

—turned sunken eyes out the window to the French curlicues on the building across 47th. Morning light pitilessly revealed four days' beard and a white salt crust under the armpit of his shirt. A wheezing grunt rocked his upper body. Wait eight seconds and he'd grunt again.

"Dad." No response. "I said, Dad!"

The old man's head wobbled around. "Stone. Glad you came by. Let me show you what I'm working on. I haven't programmed a movie this good since *New California*." His left hand shook as he touched the screen. The spiral vanished, revealing a litter of icons and a dozen overlapping windows. "Where the hell is it?" Another grunt. "I'll show you later."

He reached for a stainless steel tumbler in the cup holder at the lower right corner of the touchscreen. His jittering right hand cradled the lid. He didn't lift it. A frown carved deep lines from the sides of his nose past his mouth. "What brings you by?"

"You didn't come yesterday."

"Come? Where?"

"My graduation. From high school. Where I've gone the last four years."

"Graduation?" Dad lifted the tumbler. "It's on my calendar for next week." He brought the tumbler to his mouth.

A decade before, when Dad's last two photorealist computer-animated movies had underperfomed compared to his earlier hits, he'd poured a cup of orange juice over two fingers of sextuple-distilled vodka every afternoon at five. When Mom left him four years later, he'd mixed equal parts of orange juice and a cheaper vodka, starting at two-thirty or three.

Now Stone would bet the tumbler contained only vodka from the empty plastic bottle lying on its side next to the overflowing trashcan.

"Commencement happened last night," Stone said.

Dad squinted at the tumbler's lid. "It was last night?"

"Do you even know what day it is?"

"Friday." Another grunt. "Right?"

He locked his body as a boiling sensation welled up his chest. Stone's eyes flicked to the window. Push the old man through the glass and to the sidewalk four flights below. Finish the job alcoholism started.

A chill shivered over his arms. He'd loved his dad, not just as a child, but as a young teen, living with Mom and beginning to understand just how badly Dad ruined his own life. If he'd shown up just once to a game, just once....

Damp warmth pushed from behind against his eyes. No. He wouldn't show Dad how much he hurt.

"Today is Saturday? Commencement was…." The hole in the tumbler's lid pulled down the older man's attention. His hand trembled, sloshing vodka against the tumbler's walls. He lowered his hand. Looked up. Red filled his eyes. A tear flowed down the wrinkles in his right cheek. "Jesus, Stone, I'm sorry, how could I have forgotten, how can I make it up to you—"

Stone's voice choked. "You can't." He yanked his gaze away, hurriedly stumbled out of the study, across the living room. Grabbed for the door.

He touched the knob and everything shifted. Night sky hemmed in by skyscrapers. Ranked white orbs of the field lights. Breathing hard, inhaling the taste of dirt, grass, chill autumn evening. So few boys had come out for football he had to play both sides of the ball. Defense now, playing free safety on the strength of his great-grandfather's name and hips.

Stone knew the play before the snap. His high school led by two with two minutes left. Ball near midfield, the other team would run out routes, its receivers instructed to get out of bounds after making each catch in order to stop the clock.

The receiver cut for the sideline and the cornerback slipped. The quarterback threw. Stone broke toward the pass. Ball high. The receiver jumped, stretched arms overhead—

Stone extended his arms. Shoved the receiver in the small of the back, bending him into a C, flinging him at an awkward angle toward the opponent's bench. The ball thumped the cold ground somewhere behind Stone. Red lights on the receiver's sensor display, a well-timed touch, clean and legal.

The receiver writhed on the ground. "Muh fuh-ing back!" His teammates gathered around.

Stone stared at his wincing brown eyes. Stone's teammates bounded up, slapping his helmet. Fingertips smudged his visor. "Good touch!"

Stone barely heard. His stare left the receiver and slashed through the visors of the receiver's teammates. Most flinched. Hell yes.

The back judge moved toward him, pudgy middle-aged authority in no mood to tolerate taunting. Stone's teammates tugged him away, still cheering his play.

High-pitched voices squealed in the bleachers. The girls would talk about him in the hallways tomorrow.

Hell yes.

Stone's senses shifted. The whites of the injured receiver's eyes faded last. Girls flowed by. Cheerleaders wearing short dresses met him at their apartment doors while their parents traveled for the weekend. College girls stinking of cannabis vape pens. Melanie, confusion and panic in her eyes. A blur of fun fearless females out to change the world, grinding away their twenties and early thirties in the heartless maw of Manhattan. Women on missions on Earth, dark skin, choppy accents, sweating stinking Third World cities blaring outside the windows, crumpled wads of US currency, thousands and five thousands, dropped on the chipped veneer of particle board nightstands. Colonial women, fresh-faced and naive on newly-rediscovered worlds, prematurely aged on planets long acceded to the Dubai Convention.

Teresa Benavides in his hotel room on Freeland, posing as the former.

A woman he'd never bedded, the keyhole kop, Caitlyn Fredriksen. Long blonde hair and hazel eyes sparkling like agates. They climbed out of *Lady Lux* canted by the uneven melting of orange rock under its engines. His left arm ached and the floor's angle made his gorge rise. The hatch opened. Australian desert air assailed him. Caitlyn gripped his forearm and helped him out. Even hotter than the air, the melting rock below poured out heat like a vent of hell.

At the horizon, a line of red hills swirled. His stomach clenched. He shut his eyes.

His nausea vanished. Cool air, dry, late winter or the first days of spring. But not New York. He opened his eyes.

A crowd gathered in front of the limestone steps of a medieval palace. Men and women in ragged wool thronged the street. Near the steps, velvet and silk replaced wool, and leather replaced bare feet. Each step held a rank of men-at-arms, swords scabbarded, shields point-down on the stone, steel chestplates and arm pieces and openvisored helmets gleaming in midday sun. On the landing above the steps, priests and priestesses, robed in blue and red, flanked a tall man, broad-chested, a yellow tunic draped over his polished armor, and a plain golden circlet on his head.

The helmet induced the logic of a dream. He was both Stone Chalmers and a common laborer, come to hear the king's speech as crisis stirred on the realm's borders.

Stone inhaled. The stench of a thousand unwashed bodies made him gag. *Push forward to the merchants. They can afford perfume. Maybe even soap—*

An eyeblink found him among the merchants. He glanced down at a jacket of green velvet and ruffled silk sleeves emerging from the jacket's cuffs. His belly strained the ample waistband of his pants. Agates adorned gold rings half-swallowed by pudgy fingers. The gemcutters and goldsmiths in his employ, now somewhere behind him in the throng, did fine work.

He looked up. The men-at-arms' shields bore a starry device: the Big Dipper's leading edge pointed at Polaris, while Venus hung low in the western—

Another eyeblink. He stood tall despite the steel mail and plate weighing him down. Uneasy looks from the nearby merchants glanced off his armor like the swings of ill-trained swordsmen. The merchants knew how much they owed the men who protected their interests. Guilt gnawed them at how little they paid. He didn't just guess from their expressions. He knew from being born among them.

Behind the merchants crowded the poor. He had trained with some of their sons, in skills that seemed dreamlike in the light of the cool spring morning, in parachute insertions and long-range marksmanship in fanciful places named Al-a-ba-ma and Ken-tuck-ee. Simple folk who worked hard to afford bread for their children and cups of watery beer. Simple folk who worshipped unexamined gods—

Blue robes draped over his stooped shoulders. The backs of the ranked men-at-arms dominated his view. No doubt Car-ter next to him studied the curves of their thigh armor with great interest. Live and let live. Car-ter kept his perversion hidden and spared the priesthood public embarrassment.

Enough of his fellow priest. His thoughts ranged to the other side of the landing. Priestesses in red robes, and smooth pale skin beneath, and all the ways a priestess could remain a virgin and a priest could get no woman with child....

The king's voice turned solemn. Rote prayers flowed from the king's mouth.

If the gods heard human prayers, they never showed a sign. But if invocation of divine favor made commoners work harder, merchants provide greater value, and soldiers fight harder, pray on.

He blinked and sniffed out a breath. Perhaps invocation of divine favor made kings more kingly—

"—and we beseech Thee, o Lords of Heaven and Earth, to guide us according to Your will, all the days of all our lives. So be it."

His final words echoed off the wall of the temple to the side of the square. He held his back straight and his jaw firm for a long moment, then turned for the front gate of the palace.

Even then, the guardsmen at the gate could see him. He kept his face and posture resolute. They couldn't see how tired he was. Barbarians to the south, civilized but inscrutable kingdoms to the east. Defeating one only meant another shrieking tribe or another foreign dynasty would rise up and raid or invade one of his provinces. And whatever policy he chose would cut at the livelihood of someone among the four estates. Schemes would enmesh him like spiderwebs, all cloaked in stirring words about the good of the kingdom, all seeking to enrich one of his subjects at the expense of others.

If only he could abdicate and take the green of a common soldier.

He strode through the gate. Everything around him lost color, lost sound.

His mouth went dry. *What's happen...*

Lost consciousness....

Stone woke in darkness. Cooling fans whirred nearby. Padded seat under him. He thought about lifting his arms from the armrest but they refused to rise.

Still under the influence of Sheila van Bentum's drug. Still in the chair.

Three-d text coalesced in front of him.

Name: Rolston Wentworth Gridley "Stone" Chalmers
Aliases: Edward Lavellette
Tobias Becker
Jasper Jezhek

The list scrolled on. Had the procedure pulled out of his brain every cover identity he'd ever used? He couldn't remember them all.

Sex, anatomical: Male
Sex, chromosomal: XY

———

Genetic markers of personality traits

———

Androgen receptor CAG repeat length: 15
ADRA2b deletion: no
5-HTTLPR variation: long

Hundreds of lines of gibberish raced up his field of view. He couldn't understand it even if he had time to read it.

Sounds. Somewhere outside the helmet. The padding of soft-soled shoes. A rustle of fabric, bodies shifting position.

The lines of gene-marker gibberish scrolled out of his vision. New text popped up, swimming for a moment until his eyes adapted to their fixed position in front of his eyes.

Gender identity: Male
Sexual orientation (modified Kinsey): 0.1 (exclusively heterosexual)

Lifetime sexual partners (female): 200 est.
Lifetime sexual partners (male): 0
Monogamous relationship suitability: very low

He sniffed out a chuckle. Sheila van Bentum's black box delivered accurate results. So far.

The words slid to the left, out of sight. New text filled in.

Stone's smirk softened. His eyebrows crinkled.

————

Personality parameters

————

IQ: 112±3

Five Factor Model:
Openness to experience: very high
Conscientiousness: low
Extraversion: very high
Agreeableness: low
Emotional stability: high

Myers-Briggs type: ENTP

O.S. Card life stage assessment: Adolescent (seeks power
and freedom, rejects belonging)

Likelihood of advance to next stage (Adult (seeks
power and belonging, rejects freedom)) within
five years: very low

V. Frankl loci of meaning:
Faith: 0%
Family: 14%

> *Work: 81%*
> *Overall sense of purpose: 83%*

In the room outside his helmet, someone drew in a long, sharp breath. A murmur. "So low?" Sheila's voice.

"For a man from Earth today," muttered a reply, "be surprised even one of the loci is so high."

A woman's voice. Had he heard it before? Where? Whose?

A third page of text appeared. Stone read. His eyebrows crinkled more. Varna?

> *Placement in Four-Category Social Alignment:*
> *Hindu varna: Kshatriya*
> *Western estate of the realm: Nobility*
> *Subestate: Knight*
> *Leadership suitability: medium*
> *Follower suitability: low*

––––––

> *Suggested careers: policeman, soldier, spy.*
> *Likelihood of fulfilling marriage: very low.*

The words hung in front of his eyes for ten slow, pounding beats of his heart.

> *Protocol complete.*
> *You may wish to discuss your results and their applicability to*
> *   your evolving quest for alignment with the universe with a*
> *   facilitator.*

A voice came to him. Sheila's. "Do you grasp what this means?"

"No."

Sheila sighed out a breath. She muttered something Stone barely heard. Perhaps "You're sure?"

If the other person in the room answered verbally, the words didn't penetrate the helmet.

Sheila spoke again, much louder. "There is another person in the room with me. You will follow this person's instructions exactly as you follow mine."

A motor hummed above him. The helmet rose, squeezing his ears against the side of his head. White light flooded his eyes. He blinked and squeezed his eyes shut. Cooling fans sounded on three sides. A delicate floral perfume trickled into his nose. Not Sheila's scent. Whose?

Stone reopened his eyes. He could tolerate the washed-out brightness now. "Turn the chair."

Servos under him slowly rotated the chair to his right. Sheila van Bentum came into view. Her eyes still showed him sapphire ice, but her tongue darted nervously between clenched lips. Her blue eyes darted to her left.

Dark pride welled in him. Not agreeable at all. Edward Lavallette turned out to be more than she expected.

The chair spun further. He forgot Sheila in an instant. A lean woman, smartly dressed in navy blue pants. Blond hair brushed the shoulders of her white blouse. Her hazel eyes appraised him.

Caitlyn Fredriksen.

How? Not a fellow passenger on *Yassir Arafat*. She must have journeyed here with the diplomatic mission, and stayed.

Forget that. Caitlyn. Once a rival, once a partner, but now…?

"Key—" He cleared his throat. "Keyhole kop. What do you want from me?"

"Stone Chalmers," she said, "I want you to help me save the human race."

CHAPTER 7

He kept his voice calm. "I save the world every day."

"Stand." Her words yanked him out of the chair. "Exit the room...."

His mind raced while his body trudged through the Center at her commands. What was Caitlyn's game? Some operatives ran side hustles, smuggling, gun-running, the like. But from their first meeting, he'd viewed her as a straight arrow who would never abuse her position.

A rogue operative wouldn't try to enlist him in a side hustle by telling him joining her would save the human race.

Stone stepped through the revolving doors. He halted on the landing under the swooping granite buttress. Although the mass of rock held traces of the day's heat, a chill ran down his back.

A black coupe with rounded lines, standard issue from the UN motor pool, pulled up and parked itself. The door on the near side popped open.

"Get in the car," Caitlyn said from five feet away. "Sit on the back seat. Do not move."

Stone climbed in, sat on gray leather. He caught his breath. Did every vehicle on Minerva have a new car smell?

Caitlyn took the front seat, facing him, and crossed her legs. Her top foot dangled six inches from his knee. Her blond hair brushed the ceiling as she looked up and spoke to the coupe. "Travel plan A."

"Where are we going?" Stone asked.

The coupe whispered out of the buttress's shadow. Stone squinted against the parking garage's stark white light. A moment later, the coupe's windows polarized. Darkness enveloped them.

"A place to talk."

"Meaning you'll talk and I'll shut up and listen."

Caitlyn raised an eyebrow. "Have I ordered you to be silent?"

He tried to roll his wrists in a shrug, but they wouldn't move. When would the drug wear off?

Wrong question. How much intel could he gather until he regained his freedom to act? "Why does the human race need saving? And what makes you the one to save it?"

"*Now* I order you to be silent until the car stops."

The coupe climbed the ramp and turned right onto the dark and quiet street. Away from the UN tower. Midrise structures loomed above empty, clean sidewalks.

After a few minutes the coupe drove through a neighborhood of single-story buildings, coffee bars and boardgaming parlors, unlit in the late evening. His implantable couldn't radio the UN tower from this range even if he were free to try. Caitlyn took him further out of range every second.

The city thinned out. To the left, a golf course undulated under the wan light of Minerva's small moon. Bunkers looked like misshapen yin-yang symbols, gray-white sand contrasting with moonshadows. Lampposts behind the golf course lined the railroad line to the space elevator. On the right, the roofs of houses on acre lots peered over a wall of grown granite facing the road.

The last neighborhoods of Euler City fell behind the coupe. Hundreds of rows of potted evergreen saplings, about five feet tall, ran perpendicular from fences along the highway into the night-shrouded distance. A sign clipped to a fence wire marked the nursery as property of Berglund Ecoseeding Company. The company's logo was a blue tree bisecting a yellow sun.

Ten minutes later, the coupe slowed. The bluish-white headlight beams showed the highway curved around a rocky mound and out of sight. The coupe left the highway, turned right onto a two-lane road. The headlights glistened on blue-black asphalt and crisp yellow dashes down the center line. Evergreens eight to ten feet tall blurred by. Pines, maybe, or firs planted by the ecoseeding company. Not potted, but wild, digging roots into thin soil. The road climbed into a range of low hills, sliced through the hills' knife-edge ridgelines.

The coupe slowed. On the left, a gravel road cut through another low hill dotted with evergreens. The car turned. Gravel crunched under the wheels as the coupe slowly continued its journey to wherever they were bound.

Five more minutes and the coupe turned left, onto a narrow lane consisting of two dirt strips separated by tufted grass. The grass brushed the coupe's undercarriage. They must be approaching their destination.

Fourteen breaths later, the coupe rolled to a stop. Muffled by the coupe's closed doors, a hundred crickets chirped outside.

Stone's body stiffened. Enough space separated the pines or firs to fit a shallow ditch, six feet long and two and a half wide. But if she wanted to kill him, why claim she needed his help to save the human race? To dull his resistance to her killing strike? Sheila van Bentum's drug did that ten times better.

Unless it wore off soon.

He tried flexing his fingers. They refused to budge. Do not move, indeed.

At least his eyes could turn to right, then left. Unless the drug disrupted his sense of direction, the future wormhole site should be no more than five miles to the left. No sign of it reached the corner of his eye through the evergreen forest, not even a light glow in the distance. His gaze paused on a small metal sign on a post along the dirt track. Blue evergreen, yellow sun, letters *BEC*.

The headlights blinked off. Darkness surrounded the cabin. A dome light in the ceiling angled toward him. Caitlyn remained in shadow. Faint sounds came from near her right hand. Assume she'd pulled a handgun from a storage cubby.

But no sound of a slide racking. She hadn't chambered a round. If he could leap across the cabin, he could strangle her before she could fire.

"Societies have life cycles," Caitlyn said, "just like people, from youthful vigor to decline and death. The ancient Hindus, Greeks, and Levantines all imagined a past Satya Yuga, a Golden Age, an Eden, that devolved to the present fallen world. Ibn Khaldun and Oswald Spengler created qualitative frameworks for thinking about societies' life cycles. Peter Turchin's innovation over a century ago lay in applying quantitative analysis to the problem. Other cliodynamicists—quantitative historians—since then have expanded on Turchin's foundation and brought in other ideas, such as James Grier Miller's living systems theory and—"

Stone's voice crackled from disuse. "Enough background."

"You don't need it. Here's what we know about society life cycles. At an early stage, a growing society has a high degree of group cohesion. As a result, the society's leaders perceive that their greatest personal gain will come if they work together to exploit their society's skills and resources. By working together, they start their society on the path to greatness."

Strangle her, but then what? Locked in a car with a dead woman until he died of dehydration. Assuming the car didn't drive him to the UN tower or Minerva police headquarters. Edward Lavallette would cool his heels in jail until long after *Yassir Arafat*'s engineers landed the wormhole mouth on Minerva.

"The Romans conquered neighbors who were too poor to defend themselves and rich enough to make worth conquering. The Americans swept aside primitive indigenous peoples and turned the temperate half of a continent into the workshop of the world and the arsenal of democracy. Perhaps it's like winning football games?"

Memories of high school practices and his coach's pep talks drifted up. Stone tested her words against the memories. Her words rang true. "I see what you're saying."

Besides, you can't gather much intel from a dead woman. The more she talked, the more she might reveal.

Especially if she meant to recruit him to her cause.

"Next question. Why don't great societies continue on an upward path forever?"

"Another society with more ruling class cohesion comes along."

"A good guess." She shook her head. "Invaders are a symptom of social decay. Not a cause."

"And the cause is…?"

"The time of greatness contains the seeds of decay. The society's leaders think the growth phase will last forever. What they don't realize is the founders built the time of greatness by plucking low-hanging fruit. Sooner or later, the low-hanging fruit runs out. The Romans ran out of easy, rich conquests. The barbarians to their north and northeast were too poor to be worth conquering, while the advanced societies of the Near East were rich enough to defend themselves. The Americans ran out of frontier and inefficient social sectors they could easily reorganize."

"Wouldn't their group cohesion make them agree to lower their expectations? Or—" How had she phrased it? "—learn new skills and find new resources to exploit?"

"Group cohesion is difficult to maintain. It's similar to preventing symbiotic organisms from becoming parasites, or normal cells from becoming cancerous. The first to defect from the group's cohesion can reap huge gains. We're getting into the indefinitely iterated prisoner's dilemma discussed by Robert Axelrod—"

"I'll take your word for it."

"Back to the society's leaders when growth becomes more difficult. The inheritors of the founders were usually born with a silver spoon and lacked the drive to work as hard as their predecessors, let alone work even harder to extract the same amount of growth. So they don't. But they still want personal gain. Where can they find it?"

"You tell me."

"Since it's too much work to find personal gain outside the society, they seek it within. Group cohesion gives way to faction and intrigue. The principles the society's founders held themselves to become empty slogans. Government goes from raising the tide to lift all boats to picking winners and losers within the society. The rulers focus on persuading the government to maintain their perks. Elites who lost out when perks were granted seek to seize the government. Both factions of the elite use the masses as pawns, then ignore them. The society rots from within."

" 'Rots from within'? Sounds melodramatic."

"You'd like concrete examples." Caitlyn ticked them off on manicured fingers. "The elites prop up the profits of their business enterprises by importing cheap labor. This threatens the livelihood of the masses, who are mollified by an ever-expanding welfare state and taxpayer-funded stadiums. The military's budget grows, but elites divert most of the increased funding to themselves and their cronies, and military effectiveness collapses. To pay for all its programs, the government increases taxes, inflates the currency, and imposes draconian economic regulations."

"Are you talking about the Romans or the Americans?"

In the dim cabin, her hazel eyes became dark pits turned on him. "Both."

Stone smirked. "So your faction is the one that lost out when the UN granted perks fifty years ago?"

"No." Her tone lacked any taking of offense. "We intend to found a new society better able to maintain group cohesion."

"The revolutionaries always say that when they grab for the brass ring."

"You think the leaders who turned the UN from a debate club into a world government founded something. No. I glossed over a stage that frequently appears in the societal life cycle. It's similar to the point in a human life cycle when a person gets over his midlife crisis. Some societies have an elite faction attempt retrenchment and restoration of the society's founding spirit."

"Meaning?"

"The Romans suffered a civil war five decades long, with twenty-five different warlords proclaiming themselves emperors. Diocletian restored order, by making the Roman government more authoritarian, more bureaucratic, and more repressive than it had been before the crisis. When Diocletian's policies and the rise of Christianity didn't solve Rome's problems, Julian the Apostate attempted to restore paganism as the state religion. The Americans about two centuries ago went through economic and social upheaval and the loss of China and Eastern Europe to Communism. The conservative masses turned to Reagan, who defeated Communism but failed to restore the former American way of life. As a last attempt to restore their way of life, the conservative masses then turned to Trump."

Stone's eyelids drooped at the history lesson.

"I'll sum up," Caitlyn said. "In both Rome and America, the restoration attempts failed, because conflict between factions proved too strong."

"The men who remade the UN as the world's government succeeded," Stone said.

Caitlyn angled her head in an *oh really?* look. "They had good luck. So far."

"Luck?"

"They seized control of the exotic matter factory—what we now call Hawking Station—and found a physicist from a small town in North Dakota, of all places, who provided the stroke of genius needed to turn exotic matter rings into semi-stable wormholes. This allowed the heads of UN member states to exile troublesome minorities to colony worlds."

"Even without the Dubai Convention—"

"They manipulated public opinion in the United States to turn a still-formidable military into a peacekeeping force ready to suppress dissent at a moment's notice anywhere around the world. They built the most pervasive spy agency in history to maintain a watchful eye on every threat they could imagine."

"You're welcome."

Caitlyn sniffed out a breath. "It won't be enough. The Dubai Convention colonies will soon be overwhelmed by the resettled."

"So what?"

"The demand for resettlement slots is increasing."

"...Increasing?"

"You didn't know that? I shouldn't be surprised. Few do."

Stone said, "The rate of colonies acceding to the Dubai Convention has slowed."

"Yes. Minerva will probably be the last one ever. But the number of

UN member states wanting to exile undesirables is increasing. Originally, resettlement had some justification. Five to ten thousand people from each of six countries suffering intractable civil disorder, voluntarily moving to new worlds without the baggage of the past. But now, two hundred UN member states want to ship out up to forty-nine percent of their populations. Call it two billion people divided among almost fifty worlds."

"Forty million each..." Stone's eyebrows jumped. On a typical Dubai Convention world, the resettled would outnumber the colonists fifty to one. No colony could feed that many resettled, and would itself starve if it tried.

"Resettlement will cease before two billion people are exiled from Earth. Instead, those two billion people will suffer the same fate as billions before them. Oppression, ethnic cleansing, genocide."

A cynical thought came to him, cloaked in leftover words of the Tobias Becker cover story he'd used on Trinity. "The poor you will have with you always."

"Don't get cute. Now, a small group with an ion exchanger, a mass spectrometer, access to seawater, and electricity from a shantytown's roofs covered with solar panels can isolate enough enriched uranium to build a twenty-kiloton atomic bomb smaller than a shipping container. A larger group with ten competent nuclear engineers can use that atomic bomb as the primary for a twenty-megaton hydrogen bomb and deliver it at optimal burst height over any city on Earth. Another small group with a protein synthesizer, a nucleic acid synthesizer, and computer software to predict interactions of viral coat proteins with cell surface proteins differing between ethnic groups can unleash a genocidal plague. Unlike the Time of Troubles, these small groups may emerge not just from the slums of Earth, but from the resettlement camps and original colonies of almost fifty worlds. Forget the Time of Troubles; the human race risks apocalypse."

Even if her dire prediction were accurate, "What can you do to stop apocalypse?"

She stared at him from deep shadow. "Our best chance is for the Minervans to spread Alignment with the Universe through the settled galaxy as rapidly as possible. If a critical mass of people learn who they truly are and where they truly belong in their society, group cohesion will emerge naturally."

"How did they ancient song go? 'You could say I'm a dreamer'?"

"It may not be a good chance, but it's our best chance. Which is why we need you."

Stone clamped down on a smirk. There were four main ways to recruit a humint asset or turn an opposing operative, known by the acronym MICE. Money? He had more than enough for his lifestyle. Ideology? Caitlyn didn't need Sheila's mind-reading tech to know he wouldn't respond. Compromise? You can't blackmail a man for sexual indiscretions when he brags about them.

Only Ego remained. Flatter the target into thinking he could outsmart the recruiter.

"What can one man do for you? Even if that man is me?"

"Keep Gray from blocking the Minervans."

Stone gave one slow blink. Gray didn't conspire with Caitlyn. Or she wanted him to think that. "Why would Gray care about the Minervans' state religion enough to stop its spread?"

"He worried enough about Minerva to send his best operative here, didn't he?"

She didn't need to know Gray sent him here to build up credit in the UN bureaucracy's favor bank. He let himself smirk. "Good point."

"You're in?"

Of course he would say he joined her conspiracy. He could only leave the car alive and free to act if he did. But she knew that too. If he agreed too quickly, she would suspect he lied. "I've struck out with every Minervan woman. If Alignment with the Universe spreads, I'll strike out with every woman on Earth."

"Don't worry. The kind of women you pursue will still throng Manhattan for decades yet."

"They're aligned with their inner sluts?"

A breath in, then Caitlyn said, "You could put it like that."

Another objection arose, carried by images of Euler City's quiet streets and the truths revealed by the Alignment protocol. "If every human being in the galaxy is aligned with the universe, no one will need a policeman, a soldier, or a spy."

"A fit and healthy person still has an immune system. Policemen and spies are a society's analogs. Even Minerva suffers from crime and disorder."

"A kid throws a rock through a window once every week?"

"Even if everyone were aligned with the universe, the settled galaxy would suffer from crime and disorder too. And don't worry, the process of aligning every human being with the universe will not end until after you've retired. You will have many more chances to ply your trade even if you join us."

He still couldn't record her treacherous words to his implantable, but after he got back to his room in the UN tower, he could record an encrypted report he would send to Gray in the first diplomatic pouch back to Earth after siting the wormhole.

Stone peered into the gloom on her side of the cabin and put on the most sincere expression he could manage. "I'm in. If I could move my hand, I'd shake on it."

CHAPTER 8

Yellow light flared on the western wall of Stone's hotel suite living room. He blinked bleary eyes and squinted to the east. A limb of Minerva's sun peaked over the horizon and its reflection dazzled off the gray-green surface of the Wisdom Sea.

"Close the blinds," he said to the suite. No harm would come if Caitlyn Fredriksen or a Minervan counterintelligence officer overheard those words. He'd swept for bugs and cameras, of course, both after first arriving at the room and when he'd staggered in late the night before. He'd found no spy devices hidden nearby, but the Minervans might have longer range monitors about which he lacked intel.

The motors hummed until the rectangle of yellow light on the far wall shrank to nothingness. The floor lamp near the wood-grain plastic desk seemed dim in contrast to the stark daylight.

Stone lolled his head back on the plush, boxy armchair and shut his eyes. A hidden camera would show a man who'd partied late and couldn't sleep. A hidden microphone would fail to pick up the dictation he subvoked to one of the encrypted memory sticks in his pocket synced with his implanted computer.

Extent of conspiracy is unknown. Subject Fredriksen multiple times used 'we,' though she might have been suggesting she has numerous supporters to increase my chance of joining her. Her travel with the diplomatic mission and assignment to that mission's stayover team suggest one or more ITB personnel are coconspirators.

Threat does not appear urgent at this time. An analyst can model spread of Alignment based on some math I don't care to understand, but my hunch is we have years before it gains enough converts to disrupt social structures on Earth or any Dubai Convention world.

I will continue to pose as a coconspirator and gather intel on Subject Fredriksen, other conspirators, and Alignment. Codename Hybrid, out.

He subvoked the command to encrypt the report on the memory stick, the one with a red stripe and raised blue bumps. The other memory stick had a turquoise band around the middle. For that one…

Spoken with heads of Minervan companies developing building materials and techniques. Scheduling meetings with heads of longevity tech companies. Numerous opportunities for profit for our agency's business partners.…

A thought tripped up his subvoked dictation. To what estate of the realm did the business partners of the UN business development agency belong? And how low were their agreeableness and emotional stability?

He pushed the thought away. *In summary, visit is on track for high success. Signed, Edward Lavallette.*

Stone locked the report on the turquoise-banded stick. He would drop both sticks in the diplomatic pouch when the communications office opened in—he checked—ninety minutes.

Catch some sleep? He could use it, but last night's events kept his nerves taut. Shower, dress, eat breakfast? His stomach soured at the thought of food. Suckered by a woman three times his age—

Flip your perspective. Sheila van Bentum's trap gave him an opportunity to gather intel on a conspiracy that almost certainly reached back to New York. How wide through the UN bureaucracy? How high?

He couldn't answer those questions from here. But other intel he could gather. Stone ordered bacon and a spinach and tomato omelet from the commissary's delivery service, then called up a map to his mind's eye.

Euler City to the east, arid evergreen forests and irrigated farms to the west. The rail line to the space elevator base ran straight from downtown Euler City for about twenty miles, then curved to the northwest. Another track ran abreast of the space elevator line for about twelve miles out of the city before curling north and terminating at a meteor crater in the middle of farmland. The crater, about a quarter-mile across, was the wormhole site.

He zoomed in. According to lidar—laser rangefinding—data from the crater floor and rim, the crater floor lay about two hundred feet below the average elevation of the surrounding terrain, and the rim rose about fifty feet above. As of yesterday's date stamp on the map, the railroad track and a parallel two-lane road ended five hundred yards outside the crater, at the start of a narrow north-south cut through the rim.

Unlike Freeland's wormhole mouth, if the equilibrator ring on this one lost containment, billions of tons of rock would shield the colony's capital city from the brunt of the gamma ray burst.

Had Caitlyn told the Minervans to do this? Or had they figured it out themselves?

He shook his head. Someone else could answer that question. He zoomed out and retraced his path from the night before. The black coupe had turned off the main road here. Turned onto the gravel road there.

The map omitted the narrow dirt track. Only a few pale pixels on the verge of the gravel road in a satellite photo revealed its existence.

Sixty or ninety seconds at five to fifteen miles per hour. Stone's eyes drew a circle on the map projected to his optic nerve. Caitlyn had taken him somewhere in that circle to invite him into treachery.

Why there?

Because she knew no one would eavesdrop.

On Earth, a handheld lidar unit could pick up the vibrations of a window caused by people speaking inside a building—or vehicle— and decode their speech from half a mile. Assume the Minervans had technology twice as capable.

How could she have known no one hostile to her cause lurked within a mile of that circle?

Stone subvoked, *I need Minervan public records of ownership and license to access*— He drew a larger circle with his eyes, radius—he made it a mile and a half.

Breakfast arrived on a wheeled robot's tray. Stone crunched crispy bacon and wripped apart wilted spinach while the search worked through Minerva's planetary network. For a society so technologically advanced in most things, the search seemed very slow. Probably an interface delay between the UN's computers and the local servers.

Results appeared as tooltips overlaid on the map in his mind's eye. Three thousand acres of the evergreen forest belonged to the Berglund Ecoseeding Company. No other legal entity or person held rights of access. Droplet Farms LLC owned thirteen thousand acres of eggplant, sunchoke, and tomato fields at the southern end of the circle, extending all the way to the north end of the wormhole crater.

A link indicated Droplet Farms contracted out ecosystem maintenance. Stone followed the link with an expectation.

Another tooltip popped up. A knowing smile curled his lips.

The farm's ecosystem maintenance was performed by the Berglund Ecoseeding Company.

Plans hatched in Stone's mind. The company's CEO would probably agree to a meeting request from Edward Lavallette. But he might know Stone's true identity and ask Caitlyn why their recruited agent had gotten curious about the evergreen forest near the wormhole. Stone would face tough questions from Caitlyn. *The UN elite don't need ecoseeding tech, do they?*

That's if she didn't write him off as a recruit to her cause and try to kill him.

Stone munched more bacon. He liked his odds in a fight to the death against her, but she could still land a lucky blow before he killed her. Especially since he'd last seen his 9mm at the Center's conference room.

And if he killed her now, his best trail into her conspiracy would die too.

He sipped ice water and an idea came. Berglund's CEO almost certainly lacked any knowledge of Stone's identity. Caitlyn possessed enough skill in tradecraft to only share knowledge with her co-conspirators on a need to know basis.

But that didn't matter. If Berglund's CEO told Caitlyn about a meeting with Edward Lavallette, then back to tough questions or a fight to the death.

Stone remembered the mission to Freeland. The head of an organization could be ignorant of what his underlings did. Reconnoiter Berglund Ecoseeding's facilities for intel? Or drive back out to the evergreen forest and scout the site yourself?

No. Assume those blue tree and yellow sun signs held embedded cameras. Assume the same signs guarded the perimeter of each of the company's facilities. Again, tough questions or worse.

And odds were he'd find nothing worth the risk of being spotted while reconnoitering in person. Caitlyn would know the UN's standard procedures for wormhole placement included subtle but pervasive monitoring of the area around the site, both from orbit and by low profile, high endurance drones able to look deep into the infrared and far into the ultraviolet. He could ask for drone data from the photorecon team, but even if he reviewed that data, he'd probably see nothing amid the evergreens and the rows of sunchokes and tomatoes.

Reconsider Berglund Ecoseeding. Why would Caitlyn want to include a bioseeding company in her plans? Genetically engineered pines and advanced drip irrigation techniques would be useless as weapons against the UN.

What other people or entities did Berglund work with?

Stone leaned his head against the chair back and composed a search request for Minerva public records. Business associates, fellow volunteers, and family members of Berglund Ecoseeding as a company and of the company's principals. He adjusted settings to anonymize the request, then subvoked *Send*.

A 3d hourglass popped into the lower right corner of his vision. Sand slid down. The hourglass flipped. More sliding sand.

He sniffed out a breath. Even if a bottleneck lay between Minerva's network and the UN's, the search should be faster than this.

A chime pinged his auditory nerves. The hourglass vanished, replaced by a text notification. *8324 results. Select report options?*

He grunted. Eight thousand results? Most of them trivial, but he had to review them all.

His wristwatch showed 0806. At 0900, the Lavallette cover had to meet with the first of today's ten Minervan technoloqy leaders.

Stone saved the search results to his implantable. He rose and stretched wiry limbs to the ceiling.

After showering and dressing, he zipped down the elevator to the UN communications office on the third floor.

His wristwatch showed 0835, yet no one waited behind the window in the opaque wall of milky glass at the comms office. He tapped his foot on milky granite and glanced around at extruded plastic tables, boxy armchairs, framed videoloops of Iguazu Falls and the tide rising around the island monastery of Mont-Saint-Michel. The vistas of World Heritage Sites didn't fit with the utilitarian decor in the room.

Footsteps behind the glass wall. A scrape as the window slid open. Glimpses of brown face, black hair. "May I help you?"

The voice sounded slightly familiar. Stone went to the window, composing his face to cover his annoyance at the delay. "Something for the first outgoing pouch. Outbound in two days?" He dug in his pocket for the first of three items. Found it. Froze.

The swarthy boyfriend of Merrill, the purple-haired pixie, scowled at him. He spat out his words. "What do you want?"

Damn her, had she confessed to him her shipboard affair? He pulled a smooth memory stick from his pocket, glanced long enough to confirm a turquoise glint. "For the first outgoing pouch."

"You stopped flirting with other men's girlfriends long enough to do some work?"

Stone exhaled. Flirting? Merrill had kept her dirty little secret. His faith in the predictability of women returned. "Sorry?"

"The party on the *Yassir Arafat* when we all watched the wormhole dock at Hawking Station?"

Stone rolled his shoulders. "I try to be friendly with everyone. Did I make your girlfriend uncomfortable?"

The swarthy man puffed out his chest. "Yes."

"My apologies to her. And you. You know, I never caught your name."

The swarthy man's scowl softened, but distrust remained in his eyes. "I am Gautam. Put the memory stick on the counter."

Stone did. Gautam's flabby arm groped to his right and pulled into view what looked like a glue gun on an articulating arm. He touched the tip to the memory stick's turquoise band, then pushed the gun back out of sight. Only a tiny black bump against the turquoise revealed the RFID tracking chip.

"Your name?"

"Edward Lavallette." Stone preemptively spelled it.

"Addressee?"

Stone made up a name and the general incoming mail stop at the Global Economic Cooperation Agency's headquarters. No special handling, no delivery confirmation. Stone stifled a yawn. Did Merrill know her boyfriend's position in UN communications meant he worked as a postal clerk?

After the final question, a hatch in the counter dropped open. Red LEDs rimmed the opening. Gautam swept in the memory stick by hand. The LEDs flashed green. The hatch closed with a faint click.

"If ITB does its job correctly, it will return to Earth through the wormhole in four days."

"Four? The wormhole drop is scheduled for tomorrow, isn't it?"

"It will take four days for the colonists to connect the transport links to the Earth side," Gautam said. His tone made clear he believed he knew everything aboout the capabilities of the Minervans. "Is this all?"

A tingle ran down Stone's arms and legs. If Caitlyn had compromised Gautam, Stone's next action would tip her off that he still spied for Gray. But to inform Gray as quickly as possible, he had no other choice.

"One thing more." Stone slipped two items from his pocket and covered them with his hand all the way to the counter. "Another stick." He requested a private connection between their subvocal microphones and their auditory nerves.

Gautam opened the connection. His expression gave little hint that they would speak without an observer noticing. Enough to fool an amateur poker player. Would it fool Caitlyn if she watched through hidden cameras?

Pick a different sender's name. Anyone from the mission directory. Odds were the random choice probably wouldn't be another member of Caitlyn's conspiracy.

What are you asking me to do?

Tag the stick with a different name. That's all.

A ponderous shake of Gautam's head. *Such a thing is contrary to proper use of the diplomatic pouch.*

Stone lifted his index and middle fingers from a corner of a US $5000 bill.

Gautam's eyebrows jolted. He inhaled deeply and set his hands flat on the counter as if steadying himself. He lifted three fingers and slid his hand until his raised fingers almost touched Stone's.

The heel of Stone's hand shoved the bill and the memory stick under Gautam's raised fingers. *This one has a different destination.*

A curt nod.

Stone subvoked over the address provided by Gray four months earlier. The glue gun added a fourth dot to the memory stick's red stripe. "It is quite simple when the same person sends two items to the same address," Gautam said.

Hamming up for any microphone that might be hidden nearby. With luck, Caitlyn and her conspirators didn't monitor audio feeds from the communications room.

Red flashed, then green, followed by a faint click.

Would knowing he was a noble or a peasant, or that he derived more meaning from faith or family, reduce Gautam's tawdry corruption? Even if the human race could be saved, Caitlyn deluded herself that Alignment with the Universe could do the job.

"Yes," Stone said. "Quite simple indeed."

CHAPTER 9

Stone returned to his suite late that night. Finally he could shuck the Lavallette persona for the day.

Not as easy as changing clothes, though. Eleven Minervans —Bradley dell'Angelo, CEO of a drone company called Light Flight LLC, had asked to move their meeting up a day—blurred together, one twenty-minute meeting after another about technologies ranging from solar-electric films to software for more rapid and more photorealistic animation. The software wouldn't have saved his father from an early, vodka-soaked grave, but Gray could use it to fill the worldnet with a hundred videos by a cover story, adding to the layers of forged digital verification UNICA's cover stories branch already knew how to assemble. On some future mission, that software might save Stone's life.

After normal working hours, maintaining the Lavallette cover sent him to dinner at a steakhouse on a bluff overlooking the Wisdom Sea, where thick glass and whispering air conditioning kept the green stink of algae from overwhelming the tang of bleu cheese and the bite of peppercorn sauce smothering his vat-grown filet mignon. Forty locals, already abuzz about the wormhole placement scheduled for the next day, came for a pitch session, taking thirty seconds each to persuade Edward Lavallette that their technologies would be valuable to Earth.

Eleven made the cut for a second round, three minutes apiece, where they spoke in smooth voices and projected uncluttered slides onto the wall behind them about how their technologies could change Earth for the better.

He'd waste half the next day speaking with the second round's five winners.

He dimmed the lights, opened the blinds onto the deep dark sky over the sea. A far cry from the glowing arrays of lighted skyscraper windows visible from his apartment back home. At least the view wouldn't distract him.

Stone rubbed his eyes. Opened the results of the morning's search of Minerva public records relating to Berglund Ecoseeding. Over eight thousand documents.

He winced. Hours of tedious work. Caitlyn could write a script to search for keywords and find any needle that might hide in this haystack.

A damn shame Caitlyn wanted to destroy civilization.

Thoughts nipped at him like a pack of stray dogs. How long had she conspired against the UN? The only answer that made sense was that she'd been sent to Minerva with the diplomatic mission by her co-conspirators. Eight months ago, and even before she, or her coconspirators, or anyone else on Earth could know what Alignment with the Universe involved. After arriving with the diplomats, she must have conspired with Alignment on her own initiative.

She held a high position in the conspiracy. How far back did that push her induction into it? Before Trinity?

Before Freeland?

He shook his head to clear the thought. Time to dig in.

First, he sifted the results to pull up names of the Berglund company's principals. Three members of the Berglund family, among them Gerald Berglund, the company's founder and CEO for decades, plus six others who were either sons-in-law or strangers.

The company name appeared in over six thousand documents. Each of the nine individuals appeared in thousands. Many duplicates. Probably most duplicate hits were company records naming one or more of the principals.

An insight pushed up his eyelids. He knew at least one other Minervan conspired with Caitlyn.

Search these results for name Sheila van Bentum.

In a blink, a summary page superimposed itself on Stone's view of the seaside window. *16 records.*

He rubbed his palms together. *Open all.*

The documents leaped out of the summary page and stacked themselves. His heart picked up its pace. He expanded the first one and read.

> *Record of Alignment with the Universe*
> *Subject: Berglund, Eliana H.*
> *Minerva Citizen ID: 4855364938851*
> *Date of Birth: 2092-11-01*
> *Date of Consecration: 2105-11-02*
> *Facilitatrix: van Bentum, Sheila L.*
> *Date of Convocation: 2110-11-05...*

Something like a Catholic's first communion record, if Catholics still practiced their faith somewhere in the settled galaxy. Sheila had pressed the buttons and spoken the ritual words when Caitlyn Fredriksen had been in diapers.

Useless.

At least there were only fifteen more documents...

...of which the next dozen proved equally useless. Sheila facilitated secondary consecration protocols when Eliana Berglund married, gave birth, and entered middle age. Next.

Eliana's father, Gerald, had served on a neighborhood association with Sheila four decades before. A scintillating document approved water slides in homeowners' private swimming pools. Next.

A company's certificate of formation. Gerald Berglund and Sheila van Bentum were two of the five owners of a company called High Emprise LLC.

Stone yawned. The intent to flip to the next document pushed toward the muscles of his throat. His eyes flicked over the document.

And widened at the company's date of formation. He stayed on the page.

Berglund, van Bentum, and the others had formed High Emprise LLC seven months earlier, less than a month after the diplomatic mission returned to Earth.

Stone studied the docoument. High Emprise LLC named its founders. Its stated purpose was *Any venture permissible under the law of Minerva.* Standard boilerplate, presumably. The certificate of formation listed a primary place of business at—Stone called up a map centered on the address—a lowrise office building on the south side of the river.

Reconnoiter High Emprise's office? Stone zoomed in on the map. The names of twenty companies smothered the building's outline like mushrooms growing on a fallen log in Central Park. At most, a shared office; more likely, a mail drop. Like any illicit enterprise on Earth, High Emprise gave the government a primary address that was an empty shell, three data sticks half-buried under dust in a corner. A site visit would garner him minimum intel for a high risk of being spotted.

What could the names of the other founders tell him?

Stone prepared another search for Minerva public records naming the company's other three owners. What were the names?

He blinked at the first one. *dell'Angelo, Bradley.* Where had he heard that name?

Earlier that day. The CEO of the drone company.

The other two names—Simon Bale and Matthew Thomas—lacked significance. Stone subvoked them and added *Search* while the back of his mind turned over what he knew.

He'd met with Bradley dell'Angelo at Light Flight's R&D facility five miles down the shore of the Wisdom Sea. In the distance, clouds of steam billowed from the cooling towers of a fusion power plant and a molecular fabrication facility. Sea breeze fluffed dell'Angelo's fine, light-brown hair and almost muffled his soft voice.

Translucent quadrotor drones darted, barely visible in the pale blue sky. They flocked like birds, wheeling together in seeming chaos but never colliding. One descended and dell'Angelo raised his hands and caught it while his upper arms stayed at his sides. A dark gray sheen of solar-electric film failed to obscure an on-board controller, lightweight batteries, and a storage compartment, now empty.

"It can stay airborne for three weeks," dell'Angelo said, "while carrying a two pound payload."

Two pounds? Enough to fit a surveillance suite of cameras and microphones. "Does it scale up?" Stone had asked as Edward Lavallette.

"Our largest model can carry two hundred pounds, remain in the air for six days, and cruise at ninety miles per hour. If you need something that big."

Back in the hotel room, Stone rubbed his fingertips on his forehead. Alignment with the Universe. Long duration drones. A bioseeding company's close access to the wormhole site. How did they fit together?

Caitlyn and her Minervan allies could launch a drone a few miles from the wormhole. Avoid detection for five minutes or less, and that drone could slip through to Earth.

A two hundred pound payload could carry a person. At ninety miles an hour, a drone could fly from the Mojave Desert end of the wormhole to New York City in a day and a half. A drone small enough to have at least a slim chance of sneaking through Manhattan airspace.

High Emprise LLC wanted to send an assassin to kill the Secretary-General?

No.

High Emprise LLC wanted to send a facilitator to—what did they call the Alignment protocol?—consecrate the Secretary-General?

Stone chuckled. Deluded colonists. Even if the Minervans could make the SecGen see himself as he truly was, the SecGen only held his figurehead position at the sufferance of dozens of power brokers. The Minervans couldn't know who those power brokers were—

Unless Caitlyn told them.

But she couldn't know all of them. Gray she knew, but the others? Stone only had hints. Someone as young as Caitlyn would know even fewer names than he did.

He chuckled. Even if the Minervans facilitated Gray's consecration,

Gray already knew who he truly was. A remorseless spider in a dark wool suit.

And even if they knew all the names they needed, the Minervans would need a dozen drones to fly unseen over a continent and the most secure city on Earth. Fat chance.

An hourglass in the corner of Stone's vision stopped spinning. Simon Bale and Matthew Thomas. Results.

He swept the business documents aside and called up information on the remaining two individuals.

Simon Bale. A photo showed calculating blue eyes. Brown scruff over his jaw and around his mouth clashed with the yellow shoulders of a suit jacket.

Stone's heart slammed as he read the dossier. Bale held the post of High Councillor of Security in the Minervan government.

The Minervan government worked with Caitlyn to overthrow the UN. Deliver that proof to Gray, and the Security Council could invoke Article 37 of the Dubai Convention, which allowed the UN to remove a rebellious colonial government from power.

He called up the next set of documents. Frowned at the photo. Did he have the right person?

Yes, Matthew Thomas. Wavy black hair, brown eyes in a light brown face. Maybe an Indian whose family took on Christian names centuries earlier.

Then Stone's eyes tracked Thomas' occupation, and thoughts of where the man's ancestors hailed from fell away.

Matthew Thomas served as Chief Scientific Officer for a company called In Vivo Biolectronics LLC, which developed nanotechnological delivery systems for implantable medical devices.

A drone developer, a med-nano guru, a Minervan government official, and a priestess of the Minervan state religion. What the hell were they up to?

More importantly, could he find out undetected by Caitlyn and her Minervan allies?

Search Minerva public records for High Emprise LLC. Real estate owner-ship and leases. Employment records.... Who worked for the company, and where. All he needed right now. More data would flood him with too much information. *Search.*

The hourglass reformed in the corner of his vision. A hunch told him it would spin for a long time. He crossed the suite's living room, pulled a bottle of sparkling water from the minifridge, twisted the cap. Plastic crackled, carbonation hissed. Then he grabbed two encrypted memory sticks from his stash in the desk drawer. Time for today's reports by Edward Lavallette and Stone himself.

...investigating company, High Emprise LLC, owned by Subject van Bentum and CEO of bioseeding company owning site of my meeting with Subject Fredriksen. Other owners include High Councillor Simon Bale of Minervan government....

He finished his report to Gray, then quickly ginned up a report from Edward Lavallette to the interstellar trade bureaucrats. He would drop the reports in the diplomatic pouch in the morning.

Ping.

He opened the search results. Scanned the data. His heart beat faster and the suite's beige walls seemed a little brighter. He knew where to go for more intel. High Emprise LLC leased a warehouse in a complex on the south side of Euler City, across the Strigidae River.

Stone threw the encrypted sticks into the suite's safe. Before he locked the safe's door, he pulled out his toolkit with energized hands.

Enough computer searching and investing time in a cover story. Time to do his real job.

Stone slung the toolkit over his shoulder and strode to the door. A chuckle bubbled between his lips.

His work gave his life its primary source of meaning? Maybe Caitlyn knew who he truly was after all.

CHAPTER 10

tone's car from the motor pool rolled out of the garage and into Euler City's cloudless night. He had ten minutes before he would arrive at his first destination. He peered out the window, but as he expected, saw nothing.

With the naked eye, at any rate.

He unzipped his tool kit. His hand went unerringly to the onyx ring. Glossy black glimmered as he passed a street light. He slipped it on his right ring finger, then leaned back against synthetic leather and rested his forearm on the bottom frame of the car window. A subvoked command instructed the ring to feed a false-color overlay of its inputs to his vision and a tone to his hearing if it saw something.

Nothing. He rolled his wrist to sweep the ring's camera over the sky on the right side of the car. Still nothing to that side.

He stretched his hands toward the ceiling. Cradled his hands behind his head.

Nothing.

Yet.

Stone reached his hands down to his shoulders and dug his fingers in like a desk jockey rubbing tight muscles.

Ding.

He slid over to the left side of the back seat and laid his right hand between the headrests. The ding returned. He turned his head a fraction to the right. A bright red line sliced through his view of the ceiling.

One ring couldn't provide binocular vision, but he didn't need to know the precise range at which the drone followed him. He only needed to know that one did follow.

He smirked and sniffed out a breath. The Minervans thought they were clever, didn't they? But even if they built drones transparent to the human eye and miserly with power, even the most efficient drone motors would still radiate waste heat.

Did the Minervans trail all UN motor pool vehicles leaving the tower? Or just his?

Stone looked out the window. The streetscape looked familiar from the night before. He checked a map of the city to confirm.

Six minutes till the car would arrive in the parking garage underneath the Center for Alignment with the Universe.

His hands returned to the tool kit. Pulled out a cardboard carton with the logos of a playing card brand and a casino in Atlantic City. Deft fingers opened the carton and pulled out its contents.

The armory techs called it a *Harry Potter cloak* for reasons unknown. Stone crouched on the floor, unfolded it, slipped it on. The fabric clung to the bare skin of his arms. Heat-absorbing rods bumped against his thigh. A message box popped into his vision. *Connecting.... done. Self-test.... done. Active mode: visible.*

He looked down at his arms and legs. Thin, transparent sleeves, rough and plasticky to the touch, hung loosely past his fingertips. A hem like an Amish woman's dress brushed the floor. After a minute, and despite being lightly dressed in jogging shorts and a moisture-wicking T-shirt, the smothering fabric already brought sweat to his armpits.

Just wait until he walked two miles across Euler City.

The car descended into the parking garage under the Center. If the nearly-invisible drone belonged to the Minervan government, and not to Caitlyn and the conspirators, the Minervan government would think that Edward Lavallette sought more spiritual guidance from Sheila van Bentum.

And if the drone belonged to the conspirators, he would at least have a chance to escape their surveillance.

The car reached the main level of the parking garage. Completely empty. The car turned left, toward the entrance to the building. Stone glanced back. Should be out of sight from any person or drone at street level.

"Stop. Open the door."

The car did as he ordered. He climbed out. Long enough since sunset for a pleasantly cool feeling to trickle under the cloak's hem and over his bare legs.

"Park and wait. Listen for further instructions on—" He named a radio channel and the car replied with a confirmation tone.

Stone shoved the door closed. The car rolled toward the nearest parking space.

Full invisibility, he subvoked to the cloak. He glanced down. Where he knew his arm to be he saw only concrete.

Maybe the armory techs knew what they were talking about for once. He slowly swept his arm in front of his eyes.

Streaks of distortion outlined his sleeve.

Stone sniffed out a black-humored breath. The armory techs always overpromised and underdelivered. Not the complete invisibility they'd promised, but it would have to do.

And more concerns than visible light faced him. A temperature gauge appeared in the corner of his vision. A standard icon, a pillar with a bulbous base. Green filled the lower fourth of the icon.

The cloak trapped infrared radiating from his body. Too much time inside and he'd suffer heat stroke.

Get moving. He activated one of the heat absorbers near his right thigh with a subvoked command, then lowered the hood over his face and walked up the ramp toward the street.

The fabric passed light inward through the hood to his eyes. The cloak's folds distorted what he saw, but Stone easily observed the streets lacked pedestrians. Infrequent cars passed without slowing.

Somewhere in the sky, too small and transparent to see and too quiet to hear, the drone undoubtedly waited for his car to emerge from the parking garage. He kept his gaze at street level and turned south at the next intersection. Above him, balconies bulged from mid-rise apartments. Drawn curtains glowed in pleated oranges and yellows.

White brightness bloomed nearby. A rectangle of light at street level. Boisterous conversations and a band playing some old rock standard.

Stone drew a breath. The open door of a bar.

Two silhouettes emerged. Streetlights resolved the silhouettes into a couple, hands intertwined, leaning against each other.

They strolled toward him.

Stone padded sideways on rubber soles. Stood rigid against stippled granite. Held his breath.

The woman squinted in Stone's direction.

Adrenaline surged through his limbs. Did she see him? His hands clenched around non-existent weapons. His eyes widened, seeking the vulnerable strike points on their two bodies, eyes and necks and kidneys. His mind raced, how to dispose of two bodies—

The woman's squint turned into a self-deprecating shake of her head.

"You good, babe?" the man asked.

She leaned her cheek on her companion's shoulder. "I am now." The folds of the invisibility cloak obscured her face on the dim street, but her voice carried a smile. The couple ambled within a yard of Stone without another glance.

He waited ten seconds, then went on, past the pub's closed door. His legs shook for a dozen steps from adrenaline hangover. The near miss soured the sweat his body generated under the stifling cloak.

Inside a pocket, the activated heat absorber softened against his right thigh.

He strode toward the river. Euler City's streets remained quiet, like a small Midwestern town after nine at night. Under the cloak, though, sweat soaked his armpits and glued his shirt to his back. Yellow floated on top of green, halfway up the temperature gauge. The rod couldn't absorb all the heat his body generated, and it neared its limit.

A gap appeared ahead between the city's midrise buildings, just as the softened rod of heat absorber sloshed into liquid inside his pocket.

He strode with purpose toward the gap ahead. The Strigidae River rustled along hard surfaces somewhere beneath street level, rising up like an overture from the orchestra pit. A wisp of cooler air leaked up from under the cloak's hem.

Even so, the temperature gauge climbed faster, through the yellow. The first sliver of red sliced across the gauge.

Stone came to a bridge. An arch sprung from the sidewalk and climbed over the river. The arch's black alloy blotted out both slices of streetlight reflections off the granite fronts of buildings across the river and a handful of stars bright enough to shine through the light-polluted night sky.

He stepped over an expansion joint between the sidewalk and the bridge. A breeze from his right, from upriver, curled over a railing and pierced a chain link fence between the walkway and the drop to the river. A suspension cable, braided metal as thick as his upper arm, plunged from the arch into a stanchion bulging from the roadway.

Sweat streamed down his face. A salty taste trickled over his upper lip.

Stone stopped even with the cable stanchion and jutted his right hip toward the railing. *Vent.*

The melted heat-absorbing rod gurgled from its pocket and out a valve in the cloak. The liquid splashed and hissed against the railing. A stink of stripped paint curled his nose.

The temperature gauge plummeted back to green.

Stone caught his breath for a moment, then activated the second heat absorber and kept going.

Fifteen minutes later, under the fluted dark green foliage of an irrigated cypress, he vented the second heat absorber across the street from his objective.

Staggered slats about eight feet high and a foot wide formed a fence around the warehouse complex. The roofs and upper walls of the warehouses peeked over the fence. The roofs slanted to the north, aiming solar panels toward the track of Minerva's bright sun. Clerestory windows ringed the warehouse walls just under the roofline.

Stone gulped at fresh air. Made a decision.

He jutted his right hand out of the cloak's sleeve. A risk, but he had to take it. He panned the onyx ring across the sky to his north.

No sign of the drone.

He resisted the urge to shed the cloak immediately and scanned the sky in other directions. Only when his scan showed the drone had not followed him from the Center's parking garage did he shed the cloak. He folded it up, laid it down under the cypress, nudged a rock over it with his foot.

Two deep breaths. A shiver ran down his back as sweat evaporated into the cool desert night. Pleasant, but he could relax after he finished his mission. Stone shrugged to reseat his toolkit on his shoulders and set out like a local on a stroll.

He studied the fence around the warehouse complex with his peripheral vision. Cameras and microphones embedded in the fence had to be watching him but were too small for him to see.

A tendril curled in his gut. Could the Minervans have a facial recognition database complete enough for the cameras to determine he wasn't a local?

As slow as the local network seemed to be, he could make it back to the UN tower before any Minervans noticed.

He circled the warehouse complex. Two hinged pedestrian gates in opposite corners. A single roller gate for vehicles stood in the middle of one of the complex's long sides. Next to each pedestrian gate, a small black box mounted on the fence looked like a biometric access control panel. A similar black box appeared to be an override for the vehicle gate control.

Trying to get in through any of the three gates would fail, and reveal his intention to the invisibly small cameras.

In his toolkit he carried a few cubic inches of shape-memory alloys and thin fabric. A parasail. Glide over the fence… if he could find a high ledge to leap from.

Where?

Stone turned away from the vehicle gate onto a side street. Even quieter than the rest of the city. Empty pavement to his left, dark windows of a kettlebell gym and a testosterone clinic to his right. Above, yellow lamps glowed behind the drawn shades of apartment windows. In this neighborhood, the apartment windows lacked balconies.

He could make it work. Find an apartment whose occupant was out for the evening. Break in without triggering an alarm or a security camera. Open a window and crouch on the sill. Jump off with enough upward force to parasail into the warehouse complex.

He winced. He could try if he had to—

A bluish-white glare bobbed against a cultured granite wall in front of him. Brakes hissed and a clattering sound followed.

A hunch fired his limbs before he could think. He sprinted across the street. Pressed his sweaty back against the granite wall of an alcove.

The light came from a vehicle approaching an intersection ahead of Stone. The vehicle's headlights swept across the clinic's windows, across where he'd stood seconds before.

He peeked out of the alcove. Sweeping curves, blue-black in the night, riding on tall tires, and an open cargo area to the back. A pickup truck. Three shadowy figures crowded the cab.

Another clatter sounded. A trailer bounced along behind the pickup's tow hitch. A rectangular cage twenty feet long, silvery and gleaming, with thin horizontal gaps near the roof, at about head height on cattle or horses. The Jezhek persona he'd used on Freeland poked into Stone's consciousness like a corpse exposed by wind scattering the fill dirt over a shallow grave. A livestock trailer.

What brought a farm vehicle into the middle of the planet's only city?

He sniffed. The trailer smelled only of clean metal. Lacked any scent of hay or manure.

The truck slowly picked up speed.

Another hunch struck.

The cone of headlights passed Stone's hiding place. He ran toward the trailer. Eyed the end of a running board visible at the back corner. Jumped.

Stone landed deftly on the running board at the trailer's rear. His grip clamped on horizontal slats and he pulled himself against the trailer's back gate. Inches below his feet, the running board held the embedded discs of radar sensors.

He sucked in a breath, held it. The radar must have picked up some reflection as he ran and jumped, but the pickup had smoothly accelerated, a sign the pickup's autopilot had dismissed his radar reflection as noise. Unless one of the figures in the pickup had happened to glimpse him as he jumped on, he could ride the trailer wherever it might go.

The pickup slowed, turned onto the street running along the warehouse complex's long side. Yet even after making the turn, the pickup didn't accelerate.

Ahead of the truck, metal and hard plastic rattled.

Stone stole a glance around the corner of the trailer.

In the middle of the slatted fence, the vehicle gate rolled open.

CHAPTER 11

The pickup veered left across the center of the street and made a wide right turn into the warehouse complex. It turned to the right. Tires whispered on fresh asphalt. Up came the welcome smells of tar and rubber. On Stone's right, a strip of grass ran along the driveway. Just beyond the grass, streetlights flared and vanished as the slatted fence flowed across his gaze. Warehouse buildings with high, dark windows slipped by on the left, like cargo ships docked in moonlight.

A growing brightness came from ahead and the left. The pickup slowed. Stone leaned away from the trailer's back gate and peered in the direction of the glow.

Stark white light glowed through a warehouse's clerestory windows. Halfway down the wall, illuminated by a spotlight, an e-ink sign named the warehouse's tenant as High Emprise LLC.

The pickup slowed further. "Truck's here!" called a man's voice outside the warehouse.

Dammit. If someone saw Stone now—

Stone jumped off the trailer to the right. Sprinted three steps over smooth asphalt toward a vehicle charging station. Crouched on the strip of grass between the charging station and the complex's outer fence.

The pickup and trailer rolled forward. Spotlights glared over a loading dock. More light spilled out from the warehouse interior through a rolled-up door in the middle of the wall. A man with a sharp nose and messy hair stood on the dock, hands in the back pockets of his pants and his gaze on the pickup's cab.

Record optic nerve input, Stone subvoked to his implantable. He peered past the man on the dock. Spindly racks of plastic or alloy receded into the warehouse interior, blurring like the stripes of a zebra herd.

He squinted. Just inside the door, two men draped black cloth over each shelf. What cargo did the racks bear? If he read the shape of the covered object or objects through the black cloth, not a man-sized drone.

Then what?

The pickup stopped. White lights on the trailer's back end flared. The pickup beeped monotonously and backed the trailer to the center of the loading dock. A man hopped out of the pickup's cab, from the side nearest Stone's hiding place, and puffed on a vape pen before the trailer's running board thudded against a rubber bumper embedded in the vertical face of the dock. The pickup's headlights whitewashed the asphalt in front of Stone's hiding place.

He froze. The men in the pickup and at the loading dock might not see him, but the glare pinned him behind the charging station. Move and they'd spot him immediately.

Stone squinted against the headlight glare. The pickup and trailer blocked most of his view of the warehouse door and the path between the door and the trailer's rear gate.

The pickup's door opened. Two men climbed out. The first, with a clipped black mustache, bowed his long neck when the second hopped down to the asphalt.

The second man looked past the other, his eyes like security cameras. The second man hadn't shaved his brown stubble for a week.

Stone's eyes widened. Simon Bale, one of High Emprise's owners and a councillor in the Minervan government.

What would the company load into the trailer?

How could he find out?

"You knew we were coming! Why aren't you ready?" Bale shouted.

Muffled voices responded. Indistinct words, but weak excuses judging by their tone.

"No more standing around!" Bale called. "Load up!"

Motion at the open warehouse door. Two human figures walked fore and aft of a spindly rack rolling under its own power. Both the black cloth and the narrow slice of his view past the trailer, he still couldn't tell what Bale's men loaded onto the trailers.

While he watched the men load the next rack, Stone slipped the toolkit off his back and rummaged inside. Muscle memory and sensitive fingers told him each item he touched. Flare gun. Rotary cutter. Flash bang grenade. A coiled forty-foot rappel line with an adhesive anchor—

Those would have to do.

Stone set the coiled rappel line on the grass near his left foot. Picked up the flash bang grenade. Small, the size and weight of a jar of hair pomade. A double activation, two buttons on the top and bottom. A slider on the side to select the effect. Four ounces, easy to throw….

He slid the switch to noise only. With his left thumb and forefinger, he pressed the activation buttons at the same time. Counted one thousand one. Threw the grenade in a high arc over the corner of the warehouse to his right. Picked up the coiled rappel line. Drew in one breath.

A *crack* echoed.

Stone ran soundlessly to his left along the grassy strip.

Men shouted behind him.

He glanced over his shoulder. Torsos twisted and necks craned away from him. He ran past the unlighted warehouse next to High Emprise's, then cut across the asphalt on nimble feet.

When the unlighted warehouse blocked the light from the loading dock, Stone slowed to a brisk walk. He caught his breath before he reached the back corner. He turned, then strode forward until he could peek at the rear side of High Emprise's warehouse.

The strip of windows at the top of the long wall gleamed with light. The pickup's headlights illuminated the charging station. Near the pickup, voices called to one another in strained tones. Simon Bale barked out commands to his men.

At the moment, no one patrolled on this side of High Emprise's warehouse.

Bale's men would need many seconds more to investigate the area on the far side. The flash bang grenade would have disintegrated, and the explosive residue should be odorless. Fifteen seconds, maybe thirty, before they reported negative findings to Bale.

Five seconds more before Bale would decide the noise could have been a diversion. Ten seconds from then for his men to follow his order to circle the warehouse.

Stone took the adhesive anchor with his right hand and held the main coil of the rappel line in his left. He padded across the gap between the warehouses. Activated the adhesive. Flung the anchor to the roof. The rappel line trailed behind, uncoiling from his left hand.

A faint splat above.

Stone tugged once. The adhesive held its grip.

He raced up the rope, pulling with his arms and walking his sneakers up the cultured granite wall. Arms only as he passed the windows—pounding the window with his feet would attract attention.

He clambered over the edge of the roof onto a black carpet of solar film. His arms ached.

No time for that. He whipped the line up from ground level. The rope burned between his palms. He winced and kept going until the line lay in a heap on the roof next to him.

From the back of the warehouse, noise. Footsteps. Low voices.

Stone lowered himself to the roof, head near the edge. He pressed the fingertips of his left hand hard against the smooth sunlight-absorbing film to keep from sliding forward and clutched the rope six inches from the adhesive with his right. He breathed cold night air deeply but quietly through a wide mouth.

Two pairs of footsteps came closer. "You seen anything?" one man muttered.

"No. What the hell made that sound?"

"Maybe a circuit blew the next warehouse over."

"You think so?"

The footsteps halted. "You got a better guess?"

The question hung for a moment, then the two men below walked away.

Once silence returned, Stone wriggled forward and peered over the edge. Nothing disturbed the space between warehouses. Out of sight to his left, men shouted and equipment rattled at the loading dock.

He ducked his chin toward his chest but only managed a steeply slanted view through the clerestory windows into the warehouse. Judging from the color, sheen, and number of roller racks inside, the warehouse held many more racks than would fit on the trailer. But what was on the roller racks?

He needed a better look. Simple to climb down ten feet of rope and look through the windows. Did he dare while Bale's men were active outside the warehouse?

No need. If they shipped out everything tonight, more trucks would come. He would only need a minute between trucks, when the men loading the vehicles would visit the toilet or the break room, to peer through the windows. If they didn't ship everything tonight, he would wait until the workmen went home and break in. Even if he tripped an alarm, the Euler City police or the Minervan equivalent of the FBI would likely conclude one of the workmen activated it improperly.

Stone sat cross-legged and coiled the rope around his ribcage.

"That's it!" boomed Bale's voice. Aluminum rang and scraped. Moments later, headlights swept across the fence. The truck rolled into view, heading for the vehicle gate. The trailer bounced along the asphalt. Even if the trailer's cargo filled its interior, its cargo weighed little.

A silence followed from the loading dock, broken by a rattling sound and the clang of metal against a hard surface. Bale's men had closed the loading door.

Thirty seconds, then Stone stood and unwound part of the rope. He peered over the edge, estimated lengths. When he had enough rope unwound, he backed his heels to the edge of the roof and jumped.

The rope jerked a grunt out of him. His feet thudded against the cultured granite a yard below the window, bounced off. He settled his feet and shifted his hands up the rope. Double-checked that his implantable recorded optic nerve data and had enough storage. Leaned forward. Looked in.

A rack stood alone in the middle of the floor with its long side facing Stone. Its shelves lacked any black cloth. A perfect view. The items on its shelves finally revealed themselves.

Drones. Translucent and small, no bigger than the one Bradley dell'Angelo had caught in his hands mere hours earlier. Each payload compartment held a tiny canister as blue as the sky over Central Park.

Drones. Four on a shelf, three shelves to a rack. Stone swallowed and turned his head to take in the entire warehouse. A hundred and twenty racks, maybe a hundred and fifty could have fit before Bale's men started moving them.

Drones. Roughly fifteen hundred of them.

Stone's arms ached. He climbed the rope and lay down on the roof to gulp more cold air from the desert night. He replayed the video his implantable had just captured from his eyes.

The cold air entering his lungs failed to dispel a burning at the base of his mind.

Fifteen hundred drones. Bound for the wormhole. Fifteen hundred drones heading to Earth. They could traverse the wormhole tomorrow, within minutes after the wormhole was sited, before work crews on Minerva and Earth could complete the road and rail links between homeworld and colony.

He zoomed in on the payloads. Cans of peaceful, restful blue, camouflaged against a sunny Earth sky.

What the hell did they carry?

The burning inside him turned to a chill stippling gooseflesh on his arms and legs.

One of High Emprise LLC's owners had expertise in medical nanotechnology.

The small canisters carried nothing good.

Stone bolted to a sitting position and rapidly unwound the rope from around his torso. Any wasted second could be fatal.

To billions.

CHAPTER 12

Stone stalked down a thickly-carpeted corridor in the UN tower. His toolkit bounced against his back with every step. Doors along the beige walls, shiny aluminum numbers in an art deco font. Room 4841… there. He halted, rapped his knuckles on brown synthetic wood, angled his ear toward the door.

Ten seconds, no sound. He rapped with quicker tempo, greater force.

Ten more seconds. Inside the room, footsteps shuffled closer. A woman's voice, soft and sleepy, clashing with the memory image of Annika Kim's high cheekbones and slitted eyes. "Who's it?"

"Edward."

As if she'd never spoken the name before: "Edward?"

Despite his hurry, old habits kicked in. Can't let a woman see you out of control. He smirked and enunciated, "La-va-lette."

"What are you doing here? At—Christ, it's 0200?"

"It's important. Very."

"In the morning."

"No. Now. Every second counts."

The magnetic locks released with a thud. The door swung open. A disheveled lock of jet-black hair dangled in front of Annika's left eye.

She sniffed and her nose wrinkled. Stone realized how much he stank of sweat from his time under the invisibility cloak.

She nodded at a yellow, floral-printed couch. The color summoned up the dossier photo of Simon Bale. "Take a seat," she said.

Stone perched himself on the edge of the cushion. He splayed his hands and tapped his fingertips together in a quick rhythm.

Annika sat in an armchair covered in matching fabric turned at a right angle to the couch. She pulled her disarrayed hair back into place and tied a ponytail with an elastic band. "If every second counts, start talk—"

A faint whine of a turning hinge, and a vertical sliver of darkness widened at the bedroom door. Her skinny, bearded boyfriend, Jordan, was it? studied Stone with narrowed eyes. "Anni, what's going on?"

"Nothing important. Go back to bed. I'll be back soon."

Jordan nodded but stayed in place. He eyed Stone with a mix of anger and fear. Not the first time Stone ever encountered that reaction.

Annika said, with emphasis, "Go back to bed."

Finally, Jordan backed out of the doorway. He swung the door most of the way closed, but a sliver of darkness remained. Eavesdropping.

Stone lowered his voice. "Thank you for talking with me. I don't know anyone else who works for ITB and I couldn't think of how else to get word to whoever needs to know."

"Know what?"

He took a breath. "ITB must abort tomorrow's wormhole placement."

She folded her arms over her chest. Her eyes turned into arrow slits. "You woke me up at 0200 for some practical joke?" She whispered harshly through clamped lips. "I thought you were man enough to not be petty that I found Jordan."

"I'm more than man enough for that. Why I'm here is a billion times more important. ITB must not place the wormhole until someone checks out what I've seen and says it's safe."

Annika squinted. "Nothing's unsafe about the wormhole site. We checked for seismic issues—"

"Not a risk of wormhole containment failure. Much worse."

"Nothing could be wor—"

"The Minervans are going to release a plague."

For a moment, her eyes flashed wide. "A plague. Really?"

"Hand to God." He chuffed out a breath, amused at the line. The producer's office seemed to lie years, not months, in the past. And he'd never reeled in Tarquinia….

Annika shook her head, bringing him back fully to the present. "But the rail and road lines will take days to connect to Earth. Without trains or buses, no disease carrier—"

"They don't need rail or road connections. They're going to deliver the plague through the air by drones."

"Drones." She rubbed her eyes, then suddenly scowled. "I said, no practical jokes."

"I'm seri—"

"How did you, some tech transfer bureaucrat whose main talent is talking to drunk women until they say 'yes,' discover this dastardly Minervan plot?"

He'd precooked a lie while parasailing from the warehouse's roof over the complex's slatted fence. "I visited a medical nanotechnology company. I took a wrong turn coming out of the restroom and stumbled into a storage facility full of drones in biohazard bags."

The bedroom door creaked. Annika scowled that direction. "Jordan, I *said*—"

"Too thirsty to sleep." He shuffled across the living room, boxers and a wrinkled tee shirt draped over his slender frame. "Don't mind me," he said through a yawn as he entered the kitchen.

Stone said nothing. His splayed fingers tapped each other more rapidly now. How long did the man need to pour a glass of water? Finally, water gurgled from the tap. Jordan emerged from the kitchen, scratching his beard, his gaze down on the glass of water in his hand.

This time he shut the bedroom door completely. Rather than guard his mate, however feebly, by eavesdropping, he preferred to go back to sleep.

Neither one of them would be happy together with two kids and a house off the Van Wyck Expressway in Queens.

Stone inhaled, focused his thoughts. An unhappy marriage lying in the future of some woman he'd seduced didn't mean a damn compared to what the Minervans threatened.

"Drones in biohazard bags?" Annika said.

"Hundreds."

"At a med nano company?"

Stone nodded.

"You uncovered their plot and they just let you walk out?"

"They were so nonchalant and they lied so smoothly about what I'd seen that they had to be up to something." Frustration ran through his voice.

She raised a stylus-thin eyebrow. "That's it? You want to call off the wormhole placement because you have a hunch the locals are up to something?"

"Not permanently. Keep the wormhole in orbit until someone can investigate."

Annika's gaze roved his face, clearly looking for a waver in his confidence. "Are you crazy? I can't go to my supervisor based on your hunch. Never mind him going to his supervisor, then her to hers, before wormhole placement ops can even tell you no."

He held out his hands. "Please. You have to. If there's even a one percent chance I'm right—"

"If."

"—how many people on Earth would die?"

She let out a breath in seeming exasperation. "Let me think on it."

"Don't think. Act. You can go to your boss based on my hunch. You know how to persuade him."

Her eyebrow sliced upward like the edge of a knife. "I do? And how would you know that?"

Stone put on a leer. A shame Jordan couldn't see it. He lowered his voice. "I've seen you up close."

Annika scowled. "I'll think on it. Now you have to go."

He blew out a breath and stood. Something in his toolkit clanked. "Don't let the deaths of billions ride your conscience."

"I'll think on it."

He read her tone of voice. A slim chance Annika would bring his request to her supervisor, let alone that it would reach the head of wormhole ops in time.

What to do? Find someone higher in the ITB hierarchy and make the same desperate pitch to them?

Stone's heart slowed and pounded like a gong. A smirk touched the corners of his mouth.

He still had ten hours to save Earth.

Stone left the room and turned toward the elevator bank. On his right, UN employee rooms along the outside of the tower. If this floor had the same layout as his, the sporadic doors to the left led to utility spaces. Exit signs marked emergency stairwells down the building's interior. Out of hard-learned habit, he kept the exit sign locations in mind, updating them as he traveled the hallway.

He mapped out his next steps. Down to the motor pool. Out to the Berglund Ecoseeding site. Find the trailers full of airborne death. He could improvise a weapon from what he carried on his back—

Around the corner ahead and to the left, an elevator door dinged. A short yet thickly-muscled man ambled around the corner, rubbing his eyes with stubby fingers. More casual than business: all the buttons of his polo shirt hung open and its tail rode over his pants. He smelled of sweat, not alcohol. He gave an amiable grunt when they passed.

Stone turned the corner to the elevator bank.

Another man waited. Despite the late hour, his gray eyes regarded Stone at full alert. He wore his polo shirt tucked and the right hip pocket of his tactical pants bore the unmistakable print of a handgun.

The hallway suddenly seemed colder. A chill shivered down his back. He'd seen the two men on *Yassir Arafat*. Security officers.

Who now stood between him and the nearest emergency exits.

"Evening," Stone said. He continued walking on a line toward the elevators, as if he disregarded the gray-eyed man.

The man sidestepped across Stone's path. Stone halted. The man asked, "What are you doing on this floor at this hour, Mr. Lavallette?"

"Calling on a lady."

"To stop tomorrow's wormhole placement?"

Stone put on a squint. His thoughts roiled. Why would Annika have called security—?

Not Annika. Jordan, eavesdropping from the bedroom. Too meek to throw a romantic rival out of his girlfriend's suite. What a pathetic, spineless—

Forget him. Talk your way past *them*.

"Stop? I tried to make the placement." He grinned sidelong. "Two foreign bodies coexisting in one spot, know what I mean?"

The man's gray eyes remained as flat as a river rock. "We heard different. Didn't we?"

"Sure did." Behind Stone, the shorter man's voice squeaked incongruously with his muscular build. He'd come closer, but not too close. About twenty feet away. Far enough to give himself time to react to any sudden attack or feint Stone might make against him.

"Here's what we're going to do, Mr. Lavallette." The first man's gray eyes glimmered. "You're going to come to our facility in the basement and you're going to stay there overnight. After the wormhole gets sited, then we'll have a talk. You'll tell us who put you up to disrupting our whole reason for coming here, and we'll check out your story. If it corroborates—" He enunciated the word. Mockery danced in his gray eyes. "—then you can go about your business."

Stone licked his lips. He could probably take them—the gray-eyed man would find it impossible to draw his pistol in time. Stone could crush his trachea and use him as a shield until he could take out the pocketed pistol and shoot the shorter man.

Did they deserve to die? Two men-at-arms, doing the king's duty according to their station?

Where did that thought come from? He'd killed better men than them on flimsier grounds.

Another thought elbowed into his mind. How long would Gray sideline him for killing two poor bastards who were only doing their jobs, when he had another option? Six months? A year?

The rest of his life?

But the other option would reveal—

—assuming Caitlyn had ever trusted him? Come on—

With a smile, Stone shook his head. "Here's what we're going to do instead. You two are going to activate Protocol Eleven-J. Then my implantable will transmit the encrypted authentication and yours will receive and decrypt it. After that, I'll walk away and you'll tell no one about our little transaction."

"Eleven-J?" squeaked the shorter man.

A head shake accompanied a roll of gray eyes. "We'd know if Lavallette were authorized to invoke it."

"Then my encrypted authentication will fail," Stone said. "Activate."

The gray eyes blinked. Through his pants' fabric, his right hand patted his pistol's grip. "Done."

"Me too," came from behind Stone.

Stone subvoked. A green checkmark appeared over the head of the gray-eyed man and a cheerful *ding* sounded. A moment later, a second green checkmark joined the first and there came another *ding*.

He tensed like a coiling spring. If these two belonged to Caitlyn's conspiracy—

The gray-eyed man's torso rocked. "Mister—Lavallette?—"

"Keep calling me that."

"We, uh, we didn't know—"

"Obviously."

The gray-eyed man raised his palms in a double stop gesture. "We'll scrub the call from our records and we'll tell wormhole ops to abort—"

"Don't bother. They won't believe you. There's nothing more you can do for me."

Their silence would prove useless. The protocol Eleven-J activation left a trail in the tower's computer network. Even though the activation record would anonymize Stone's role, if Caitlyn or her cronies received a notification that someone had invoked the protocol, she would infer that only he could have requested it.

"Excuse me, gentlemen." He strode toward the elevator. The gray-eyed man stepped out of his way. The door opened as Stone approached.

"Motor pool." His voice echoed off the walls of the elevator car. The doors slid toward each other. "Wait!"

The doors stopped, half-closed. Through the space, he called, "You *can* do one more thing for me."

"Yes, Mr. Lavallette?" said the gray-eyed man.

"Give me your sidearms."

Whispered debate ensued between the two security men. The debate ended with them both extending their pistols butt-first toward Stone. He took them one by one, studied them with a single glance. Standard UN rent-a-cop issue, plastic and stamped steel, 9mm with a fifteen round magazine, and heavy triggers designed to keep improperly trained men with fingers habitually inside the trigger guard from accidentally shooting.

He double-checked the safeties, then dropped the pistols in the loose pockets of his jogging shorts.

Thirty rounds and ten hours to save the Earth.

More than enough of both.

CHAPTER 13

Twenty minutes found the golf course and the last houses of Euler City receding behind his sedan from the UN motor pool. Instead of turning right at Berglund Ecoseeding's evergreen nursery, Stone headed down the highway past the intersection. "Slow."

The car obeyed. Stone studied a map projected into his visual field, then blanked it with a subvoked word. The headlights tracked the highway's curve to the right around the rocky mound.

He glanced out the rear window. The mound blocked from his view the intersection and the side road leading to his meeting site with Caitlyn—and, presumably, also leading to the staging site for High Emprise's plague drones. No glint of headlights behind him. He took another look. Nor in front.

"Pull over."

The car rolled to a stop on the highway's wide, paved shoulder. It cut its headlights, plunging the terrain into a moment of extreme darkness. Stone crouched on the floor in the center of the cabin, as far as he could get from the infrared eyes of any Minervan drone that might have followed him, and slipped the invisibility cloak over his head and arms.

Just an ITB employee, heading to the wormhole site on some last minute errand, stopping for some embarrassing purpose. That's what the Minervans should think if they matched this car to the motor pool request Stone had forged.

He told the car to open the door on the right side, away from the main lanes of the highway. Five thousand stars shone as clear and cold as Siberian diamonds in the cloudless sky. The cloak's stifling interior would be pleasantly warm, at least at first, in the desert night.

Stone lifted his toolkit from the rear seat, then slipped out of the car. His sneakers padded on smooth asphalt until he turned for the rocky mound. As he climbed, pebbles skittered from his sneakers and trickled downslope.

He took one step over the crest and sat cross-legged next to a thorny bush. He draped the back of the invisibility cloak onto stunted branches, careful to keep the fabric from tearing. Chill night air lifted sweat from his back. The next-to-last of his heat absorbing rods remained firm in its pocket against his hip. The temperature gauge visible in his mind's eye still showed green. For now.

The cooling provided by the night would extend the time he could wait.

He opened the toolkit. The fingers of his right hand found the object he sought. He squished a soft one-inch cube, stroked his fingertip over the activation button. Starlight cast a sheen on the cube's shrinkwrap.

Stone slowly breathed pine-scented air and kept still. He looked past the potted evergreens across the side road. His gaze hovered on the diffuse smear of light rising from Euler City above the eastern horizon.

Twenty minutes passed before blue-white light glinted behind a roll in the terrain half a mile away. Headlights came into view. The array of potted trees diffracted the glow. A distant, bouncing rattle reached Stone's ears.

The vehicle slowed. Stone ducked his head. Excess fabric from the cloak's cowl slid down his face and pooled over his breastbone.

The vehicle turned to its right, his left. The cloak distorted the vehicle's outline and its headlights blue-white glare. A moment later, the glare began to diminish.

He snapped his head up. Whipped the cloak back with his left hand. An extended cab pickup pulled a trailer twin to the one he'd ridden into the warehouse complex.

Stone squeezed the activation button on the cube with his right index finger. Tossed the cube in a low arc onto the trailer's roof.

The truck and trailer proceeded to the north. Stone scrambled over the crest of the mound and jogged back to his car. He climbed in and shucked the cloak while his implantable projected a map into his vision.

Three-eighths of a mile to the north, out of sight behind the first of the parallel ridges crossing the side road, the truck and trailer drove onward.

The tracking beacon in the small cube functioned properly.

Stone tossed the invisibility cloak into a corner of the cabin. He panted three, four breaths of cold air from the vents. No more time to waste.

"To the wormhole site," he said.

The car's headlights illuminated the empty blue-black asphalt ahead. The electric motor engaged and the car pulled from the shoulder onto the main lanes.

Five minutes later, the car took a flyover ramp suspended above empty desert onto the highway to the wormhole. The ramp descended to a divided highway, pristine and empty of traffic, like a freeway leading to one of the planned-cities-turned-ghost-towns that dotted the Third World. Five minutes after that, a concrete barrier narrowed the carriageway to one lane. The car coasted to a stop at a robotic arm extending across the road. The concrete barrier held the arm's pivot and connected at the back side with a mesh fence eight feet tall and topped with coiled razor wire. A sign on the fence next to the concrete pillar read *United Nations Interstellar Transport Bureau Wormhole Infrastructure Division. No Trespassing.*

A robotic camera on a telescoping arm emerged from behind the barrier and extended toward the car window. Stone opened the window and stared at the microphone.

"Name?" asked an artificial female voice.

Stone grinned. Robots had one advantage over human security officers. Robots didn't question when an operative invoked Protocol Eleven-J.

The arm swung up. Stone drove in.

Construction trucks and stacks of alloy trusses loomed on both sides of the highway. Plastic zip ties as thick as his arm lashed the trusses together and secured backhoes and front end loaders to the main bodies of their vehicles. Battening down the hatches before fusion exhaust descended half a mile ahead, beyond the reach of his headlight beams.

After the last parked construction vehicle, the highway continued toward the crater. To the right, a wide strip of dirt, gouged from Minerva's thin topsoil and grooved by hundreds of knobby, man-high tires ran perpendicular from the highway. "Turn there."

The car stopped on the highway like a skittish donkey. The electric motor turned off.

The hell? Ah. "Turn off transponder assistance. Switch to full self-driving."

Transponder assistance required formed in his vision, red letters against a black box. *Full self-driving mode disabled.*

Stone squeezed his forehead. Dammit. The UN limited its personnel to only routes it had mapped.

He grinned. *Most* of the UN's personnel. He spoke again to the car.

Double dammit. The UN's cars failed to respond to Protocol Eleven-J.

So be it. He exited the car and slung his toolkit onto his back. Tapped the pistols through the fabric of his shorts. Both there. Then he scanned down a mental checklist, nodded to himself. Nothing else he needed from the car. "Go home."

Travel without you? Please confirm.

"Confirmed. Go."

The car backed into a three-point turn. After the headlights turned away from him, Stone pivoted to the north. A faint breeze sighed over rocky ground, heightening the night's chill over his bare arms and legs.

Beyond nearby clumps of cactus and thorny brush, the crater poked its jagged rim toward the stars.

He checked the map in his mind's eye. The truck and trailer had stopped moving, somewhere up the gravel road five miles beyond the wormhole site.

Time to get going.

Stone took loping strides onto the dirt track. He aimed his feet at the deepest ruts, the ones most traveled by the heaviest vehicles. Compacted dirt gave firmer footing and reduced the impress of his shoes. He passed stacked drums labeled *bioasphalt - biodegradable packaging*. The smell of tar wafted through the cool night air.

The dirt track curved to the right, where stood the main formation of parked trucks.He turned left, onto hard ground, toward the wormhole.

His destination might be five miles as the crow flew, but on foot lay even more distant. Near the wormhole and the construction site, an area both UN personnel and Minervans would pack in the morning, he wound his way around tufts of brittle grass and thorns jutting from cactus. Someone skilled at bushcraft could track him like a Cape buffalo if he blundered across the terrain.

Half a mile north of the wormhole, low to the ground, a haze shimmered faintly in the starlight. Stone moved closer. The haze resolved into a six-foot chain link fence crossing his path. Beyond, narrowly-packed stripes of darker ground ran from the fence into distant darkness.

The farm between the wormhole site and the evergreen forest where the Minervans staged their drones of death.

Stone stopped at the fence and kneeled on dusty ground. He spat on a link and listened for a sizzle. Silence.

Good. Not electrified.

He dropped his toolkit off his back and reached inside. Pulled out shears with diamond blades. Snipped a link at ground level.

More silence. No alarms. At least, none here. Perhaps in a security office or police station miles away, where a bleary-eyed dispatcher would send an officer out in the morning.

He cut more links. Shook his head. Most colonies had ramshackle law enforcement. Minerva bore little resemblance to most colonies.

Could he get across the farm in time to avoid a local policeman?

The pistols tugged down Stone's pockets. A local policeman wouldn't stand a chance. Some poor bastard doing his job, ignorant of the evils that Caitlyn, Simon Bale, and the others prepared to unleash, would have to die if he did his job too well. A shame.

Stone finished cutting a flap in the fence, then pulled it back and crawled through. He yanked his toolkit through, strapped it to his back, and stood.

Rows of slender plants crowded him. The highest leaves blocked swathes of stars. Only a pulsing red target projected onto his vision by his implantable showed the direction to go. He pushed forward between two rows and rough leaves brushed his bare arms. A humid smell drifted up from the bases of each stalk, where green LEDs pierced the shadows cast by the leaves and made irrigation pipes, drip valves, and data cables glow as if seen in night vision.

He couldn't identify the plants and didn't care. He pushed on.

The rows veered to the right and climbed a contour in the rocky terrain. The target crept to the left across his vision until it lined up with his shoulders.

Stone peered ahead. The massed stalks denied him a view of the end of the rows. His low-visibility passage between the rows would have to end.

He sidestepped up sloping ground to his left. A leaf's point scratched his upper arm. Fortunately the stalk straightened back up when he entered—

Another space between rows. He sidestepped through again. Again. Again—

He broke through into a clear strip about eight feet across. The clear strip ran lengthwise along the sharp edge of a ridge, a feature of Minerva's pre-terraforming not eroded by a few decades of wind and rain. Rows of the same plants followed contour lines on the opposite, downslope side of the ridge.

Stone's gaze snapped up. Thousands of stars blazed. He glanced north, west. Part of him sought the Big Dipper, Polaris, and the evening star. Failed to find them.

He shook his head. Sheila van Bentum and the icons of her non-religion didn't matter a damn. He had work to do. Billions of lives to save—

You don't care about those lives and you know it.

Stone squinted into the darkness. A cover story flashback. Maybe traces of the Jezhek persona from Freeland, or the Becker one from Trinity, had survived removal after their missions and leaked out of his subconscious now while adrenaline and lack of sleep distracted him.

He shrugged and crossed the ridgeline. He did care; those lives were useful to him.

A bubble of disdain burst on the surface of his subconscious.

He snorted out a breath as he sidestepped across the first row of plants on the downslope. People were useful to him. The women in their twenties, yes, for the obvious reason, but many more. The techs in the armory and cover stories branch who equipped him for missions. Gray for providing a fig leaf for his naked pursuit of the thrill of action.

Hell, even Manhattan's teeming millions were useful. The kettlebell trainer at his gym. The wizened old Korean man who ran the hotdogs-with-kimchi cart on the corner. The men and women who maintained his building, hauled away trash, cleaned the streets.

Beyond that, how many billion people contributed to the economic web supporting him in First World luxury?

He pushed aside stems that sprung back at him, swatted rough-edged leaves at his face.

And how many of those billions would become even more useful to him if they found their varna, their estate of the realm?

He stopped between two rows of plants and stretched his arms to the sky. Eyes closed. Head leaned back. Breathe in. Breathe out.

Stone opened his eyes. The stars above glittered coldly.

Earth's billions couldn't grow more useful if Caitlyn and her fellow conspirators killed them.

Forget all this philosophy. How much and why he wanted to stop Caitlyn and the others paled compared to his purpose in life. He was born to kill people and break things.

Partially veiled by the rows of plants in front of him, the red target pulsed about three miles away.

Make it to the target and he would have a chance to fulfill his purpose.

CHAPTER 14

The eastern sky still lacked any hint of dawn as Stone crawled between pines up a slope. Needles brushed his face and an evergreen scent filled his nose. A cone fell nearby, hitting a rock and sending a crack echoing through the trees.

He froze, listened. Only insects and small animals made noise nearby. From ahead came far more interesting sounds. The clang of equipment. The calls of men to one another.

He reached the crest and peered over.

The ridges in the landscape ran parallel and about two hundred yards apart. Beyond the next one, a red arrow aimed downward at a valley hidden from his sight. Red glimmered over the pines beneath the arrow, like the glow of a forest fire.

Target marker off, he subvoked to his implantable. He no longer needed directions to the drone launch site.

The red arrow vanished. The glimmer remained.

Not from fire. From worklights scattered around the launch site, to give Bale's men light enough to work by while still keeping their night vision.

So much for strolling into the launch site unseen.

Stone glanced to the east. Checked his watch. An hour before dawn. Perhaps thirty minutes before twilight would render moot the night vision of Bale's men by exposing him to the naked eye.

Had Bale's men already detected him with augmented senses? No sign of it. According to the onyx ring on his finger, the sky lacked the heat signatures of airborne drones and the forest around him lacked active sensors. He'd listened for armed men patrolling the woods and heard only the hoots of owls and the skittering of small creatures in the undergrowth. He seemed to be secure here.

But from here he couldn't see the drone launch site in the valley. Let alone stop Bale's men.

He eyed the next ridge. Just a hundred yards from the site. Could he make it there while remaining unseen? And stay unseen while he reconnoitered the site?

In his mind he ran through the items in his toolkit. An idea erupted. He smiled to himself in the starlit gloom, then crept downslope.

Three minutes to the bottom of the valley. A gully wound across his path. Dry but for the black splotch of a nearby puddle shadowed from starlight by tree cover. He kneeled in the gully with a thick-trunked pine providing further cover in case Bale's men looked his way from the ridgeline.

A mosquito bit his neck. Stone swatted at it, but broke off before his hand smacked against his skin. The mosquito buzzed away from the motion.

Stone rubbed the bite against his shoulder and silently cursed. For all their advances, the Minervan ecological engineers couldn't omit mosquitoes from their artificial paradise.

Back to work. From his toolkit he withdrew the folded invisibility cloak. Only two heat-absorbing rods left, but he wouldn't need them. He pulled from another pocket the parasail. Now, a compact mass of collapsing spars folded into eight-inch lengths and sleeved by thin strong sailcloth. But soon….

Soundlessly he straightened the spars length by length. He found his toolkit knife and sliced the sailcloth off the spars, hunched over his work with his back to Bale's men to muffle the sound of fabric tearing. More knifework gave him strips of sailcloth. He tied the strips around the spars to form a low wedge shape about three feet wide and four long.

Next, he draped the invisibility cloak over the wedge, tied it to the frame of spars, and crawled underneath. With luck, the open end of the wedge would let in enough cool air to keep him comfortable if his observation lasted long after sunrise.

He snaked his binoculars' fiber optic stalks over the frame crosspiece and under the cloak at the wedge's point. Tightened the strap cinching the binoculars' cups to his eyes. The pines upslope from him formed deep shadows against the red glow suffusing from the launch site.

Stone activated the cloak's invisibility and infrared blocking functions and crawled upslope. He pushed the frame by the crosspiece and slowly picked his way over grass and pine straw, avoiding rocks that might clank and brush that might rattle with his motion. The ground jabbed the pocketed pistols into his hips.

He cocked his ear for sounds from over the ridge, checked the binoculars for Bale's men. Nothing to see. Only the sounds of men and equipment working in the next valley.

Ahead, a dwarf pine sprouted from a crevice in the ridgeline, a yard from a scruffy shrub. He nudged the left corner of the wedge against the pine's roots and stopped. The right corner nestled soundlessly under the shrub's coiled branches and needle-like leaves. The lenses on the fiber optic stalks peeped over the crest. Through the forest on the next ridge, twilight paled the eastern horizon.

He raised his hand to his temple and worked controls. The fiber optic stalks peered downward into the valley.

A camouflage net hung taut over a clearing of sparse grass and pebbly dirt. Red globes dangled from the net, providing light. The net covered the truck and trailer, which were parked next to a canopy about twenty feet square and eight feet off the ground. Some of Bale's men guided roller racks down a ramp from the back of the trailer to the ground. More men unloaded drones from the racks and carried them away from Stone and up the far slope of the valley. Closer to his observation post, a large number of empty roller racks leaned against trunks or lay sideways on pine straw.

Stone quickly counted a rough fraction of the empty racks and multiplied to get a full estimate. A hundred-twenty-five, give or take ten. Which meant the trailer had likely made its final trip from the warehouse.

He panned over two men who looked like security personnel with holstered pistols at their hips standing at an SUV's open cargo hatch. They looked to be watching monitors set up inside.

Stone's heart beat a little faster. Checking the perimeter, but they hadn't found him yet. He aimed the fiber optics at the canopy.

Another red globe hung from the center over a sitting area of folding chairs. The red globe yielded enough light for Stone to identify four people, seated, conversing. Simon Bale stroked his beard. Bradley dell'Angelo ran one hand through his feathery hair, then dropped his hand to join his other in his lap. Despite khaki cargo pants and a matching shirt, Sheila van Bentum's mound of blond hair identified her.

Caitlyn Fredriksen crossed her long legs and listened to the Miner-vans with a thoughtful look in her hazel eyes. Her conscience wrestling with the cognitive dissonance of believing she would save the world by killing billions?

He shook his head, refocused. He pegged the distance to the canopy as seventy-five yards. Three times the effective range of his pistols. He would have to get closer. At twenty yards he could charge in, put two rounds in each person's chest, and sprint upslope before Bale's men reacted.

He panned around the clearing. Enough predawn light percolated through the pines for him to count Bale's men. Fifteen workers lacking visible weapons, and five armed men, the two at the SUV and three others patrolling the clearing. Get out of the perimeter, stay twenty-five yards ahead of the guards, and sneak into the wormhole site where he could invoke Protocol Eleven-J.

The plan might work.

A bird chirped. Another of its species answered. A sliver of sunlight touched the tops of the tallest trees on the far slope of the valley.

But how to infiltrate without camouflage in daylight, with two dozen pairs of eyes and ears in the area?

A diversion? He'd used his only flash grenade the night before.

Wait till the wormhole tugs descended through the atmosphere? The roar of spaceship engines and the distorted sphere of the wormhole itself just five miles away would attract everyone's attention. Bale and the others wouldn't launch the drones until the wormhole mouth rested on Minerva's surface. He had time—

One of the security men from the SUV, his hair sandy blond and his tactical pants wrinkle-free, came into view under the canopy. He stopped in front of Bale with his back to Stone. Presumably the sandy-haired man spoke to his superior, words inaudible from Stone's distance. Bale looked up and a sour look scrunched his mouth. He nodded once. The sandy-haired man tugged his earlobe and hurried from the canopy.

Stone's mouth turned dry. He tracked the sandy-haired man back to the SUV. The man said something curt to his comrade. The two returned their attention to the monitors in the cargo space. The same low alert level as before, the only change being the sandy-haired man's toes now tapped the dusty ground. Zooming out showed the other guards continued to patrol at the same level of alert.

Stone zoomed in on the canopy. There things had changed.

Bale, on his feet now, towered over Caitlyn. His fists pressed against his hips, his elbows jutted out. His shoulders and head bobbed from vigorous speech. Stone saw his mouth from too sharp an angle to read his lips.

Amusement danced in Caitlyn's hazel eyes.

Bale leaned toward her. Spoke again.

Her hazel eyes turned cold. Caitlyn uncrossed her long legs and stood. She twisted her lithe upper body over Bale's jutting elbow and moved her mouth close to his ear. She gestured toward Sheila, who replied with an uncertain series of quick nods.

Bale pivoted to Sheila. His body language suggested brusque speech.

Sheila flinched, then lifted her chin and stared in the direction of Bale's eyes. Her mouth moved in what might have been *Yes*.

Bale held his position for a second, then shrugged. His hands opened and fell down his sides. Everyone returned to their seats.

What the hell just happened? Stone studied each face, but the argument seemed to be over.

He zoomed back out. The guards continued their patrol, their monitoring.

All normal. In front of his position.

Stone pulled the binoculars off his head and rotated his body in a half-circle under the invisibility cloak. Pebbles nibbled at him through his clothes. When his head poked out the back of the wedge, he darted his gaze around, then held still and listened. Only animal sounds. Only a small black bird moved, winding among the pines.

He swept the onyx ring across each patch of sky visible between trees. Bale's men failed to observe him from above.

Stone turned back around and watched the site through his binoculars while he listened for the motion of men behind him.

Minerva's sun climbed the eastern sky. Flying insects buzzed under the invisibility cloak, drawn perhaps by the trapped heat from his body. Something crawled along his nape. He reached back and pinched. A carapace crackled and goo squirted onto his fingers.

He continued to watch. The workmen guided the last empty roller racks into the heap amid the trees downslope. Three racks leaned together against a pine just twenty yards from the canopy. The racks left a space at the base of the tree large enough to hide a man. The guards patrolled. The two security men watched their equipment inside the SUV.

Stone's gaze tracked a path from his location to the three racks, by way of broad tree trunks, a lumpy gray boulder, and shrubs within the undergrowth. If he went quickly when the wormhole descent distracted the security personnel and the workmen, he could reach the hiding space under the three racks. Close enough to sprint to the canopy and kill Caitlyn and the others within ten seconds. He only had to wait for the descent.

From the east thumped metal and rubber. A car door.

He turned the lenses that direction. The forest and an intervening ridge or two hid the vehicle.

Who drove up? One or both of Gerald Berglund or Matthew Thomas, the other two owners of High Emprise LLC? No. Their car would have rolled to a stop next to the canopy. More security men to block the dirt track leading to the clearing? Or the car might carry some fun-seeking Minervans driving toward the wormhole site to get a better view of the descent, who ran into a roadblock Bale's men might've set up hours ago.

Stone clenched and relaxed the muscles in his arms and legs to loosen stiffness. His body handled stakeouts better in previous years. No help for that. He had to wait until the wormhole provided a distraction.

The morning warmed. Animals made less noise in the brush around his hiding place.

He waited. And waited. And—

Men in the clearing stopped work and looked high in the western sky. The guards did the same. Their hands dangled past their holsters.

Stone craned his neck. Despite the blurring effect of the cloak, a pinpoint of light reached him. He angled his ear that direction but no sound came. The wormhole tugs approached but had not yet entered Minerva's atmosphere. A thought flavored by traces of the Becker persona told him he had thirty minutes before the wormhole reached the crater floor.

The corners of his mouth curled up. Bale's men milled about with bent-back heads. He wouldn't need to wait that long.

Bale rose from his camp chair and cupped his hands around his mouth. "We're not spectators! Get to work!"

Workmen lurched up the far slope, toward where the unloaded drones must be waiting. The guards drifted after the workmen like sheepdogs behind and flanking a flock. Apparently they only expected a threat to come from the UN personnel crewing the wormhole site.

Stone turned the lenses toward the SUV. The two security personnel still watched their monitors, except when they stole a glance at the descending wormhole.

Bale's men wouldn't know what hit their boss, Caitlyn, and the others until long after Stone fled into the surrounding forest.

Binoculars back to the canopy. Bale stood, watching the workmen, his back to Stone's vantage point. The other three joined him and looked in the same direction.

Stone's heart thumped. A predator poised to pounce. You could shoot a person in the heart and lungs from the back as easily as the front.

He glanced over his shoulder. Nothing but trees, shrubs, and rocks.

Stone uncinched the binoculars. Slipped the pistol from his right pocket and worked it between his chest and the ground. A stamped steel corner poked his pectoral muscle. He chambered the first round with his left hand controlling the slide backward and forward. A faint click muffled by his body's mass. He thumbed off the safety. Returned the pistol to his pocket. Repeated with the other firearm.

Final scan of his path. All clear.

Go.

He crawled backwards from under the invisibility cloak. Still on his belly, he went to his right, behind the shrub.

He grasped a coiled, woody root with his left hand, then reached his right hand past the shrub, over the crest—

A semicircular chorus of semiautomatic rifle slides jacked cartridges into chambers behind him. A crisp male voice said, "Chalmers. Freeze."

CHAPTER 15

Stone froze. His gaze remained over the crest, and the thick-trunked pine he'd planned to crouch and run to. Twenty feet away, but might as well be twenty miles.

How the hell had they detected him? How had he missed seeing them when he'd checked the area behind his hiding spot?

One breath pushed the questions away. How they found him didn't matter. Only completing the mission mattered now.

He lay prone, his outstretched right hand about four feet from the pistol in his shorts pocket on that side. His left hand still gripped the root near his shoulder, much closer to his other pistol.

Draw with his off hand, roll over, aim, and fire at five, six, seven men who would fire back at any sudden movement? He'd be lucky to hit one before multiple rounds punched through his chest. Gray didn't pay him enough to die for no reason.

Did Gray pay him enough to die for any reason?

New thoughts. The men behind him wanted him as a prisoner, not a corpse, or else they would have killed him already.

A gleam tightened in his eye. He would have his chance to complete the mission.

"Hands slowly to the top of your head," said the crisp voice.

Stone palmed his scalp with his right hand, then overlaid his left. "Stand."

He propped his head up on his elbows, rose to his knees, climbed to his feet. Amid the trees below, motion at the canopy. Caitlyn and the other three watched him. Bale spoke to her, words inaudible—

"Face my voice."

Three steps with each foot turned him around. His face fell and his eyes darted over pine trunks and undergrowth. Six men, at most ten yards away, but where?

A camouflage-patterned mannequin suddenly appeared. Body-builders might think his build was undermuscled, but if they did, they'd be fools. Its right hand kept the muzzle of rifle shape of the same pattern trained on Stone's chest while its left lifted a pliable mask from its face. Wide-set green eyes regarded Stone from a face smooth yet rigid as a marble statue of a youthful demigod.

Stone cursed inside. Military concealment must be yet another technology where Minerva had overtaken Earth.

"Pat him down."

Movement glimmered to his left. One member of the squad suddenly turned blaze orange, like a hunter entering the woods in deer season, and slung his rifle over his shoulder. The orange figure moved silently over the rocky ground. He topped the crest and approached Stone from behind.

Tension fired in Stone's legs. Grab the orange figure and use him as a human shield? Then what? At least four or five other armed men stood in front of him… and how many others had sneaked behind Stone while he'd faced the unit leader?

Let them take you where you want to go. Then take your chances.

The orange figure pulled the pistols from Stone's pockets and tossed them to the pine straw near the unit leader. He did the same with the toolkit. Then he patted Stone down further, pulling his buttocks apart and tracing the outlines of his genitals through the jogging shorts.

Stone winced. "At least buy me dinner first."

The orange figure and the unit leader stayed silent. Not just well-equipped, but disciplined too. But had they ever fought an actual battle? Unlikely.

The blaze orange figure stepped back, faced Stone. The leader nodded. The blaze orange figure returned to his place in the semicircle.

Suddenly, at what Stone presumed came as the leader's unvoiced command, everyone's coloration transformed to camouflage. The unit leader and four soldiers. Four of them, their faces still masked, formed a diamond shape around Stone, two flanking, one ahead, one behind. Close enough from Stone to contain him, far enough away to have time to react to an attack.

The unit leader's wide-set green eyes drilled into Stone. "Turn around. High Councillor Bale and the woman from Earth are going to talk to you."

Stone turned. He glanced up at the blazing dot. So distant that the drives of the individual tugs blurred together. Twenty-five minutes till wormhole placement. Not that placement would provide him with a diversion anymore. Now, placement was a time bomb. The moment the tugs detached from the equilibrator ring, Bale and the others would release the death drones.

He walked down the slope toward the canopy. His gaze roved the woods and the clearing for clues he could use. The workmen could be ignored. The security guards too—they looked relieved when they saw the soldiers in the camouflage body suits.

Stone couldn't ignore the soldiers. Well-armed and well-trained, they surrounded him like camouflaged phantoms. When he walked to put a tree between him and a flanking soldier, the soldier would adjust his pace to keep Stone in view as much as possible, and the other three watched him every moment their comrade didn't.

They entered the clearing. The unit leader stalked through the last undergrowth and across patchy grass. He saluted to Bale, who stood just outside the canopy, wearing sunglasses against a patch of bright Minervan sunlight.

Bale returned the salute. "Have him come forward."

The unit leader tossed the toolkit under the canopy, then gestured to Stone like a traffic cop. The soldier in front of Stone moved to the side and covered him with his rifle muzzle. Stone stopped in front of Bale.

The High Councillor smoothed his beard and chuckled. "You misjudged him, Ms. Fredriksen."

Caitlyn emerged from under the canopy. A broad-brimmed, camouflage-pattern hat shielded her fair skin and blond hair from the sun but failed to obscure her hazel eyes. Her gaze measured Stone while she replied to Bale. "He's a talented and ruthless operative. He was worth recruiting."

"It was a security risk. I only allowed it in the spirit of cooperation." Bale's sunglasses made his expression unreadable.

"Not much of a risk, was it? Your men caught him." Her gaze swung to Stone's face. "He failed to alert Earth."

Stone kept his poker face. If she didn't realize he'd thrown a report into the diplomatic pouch, he would leave her ignorant.

"True enough." Bale smoothed his beard. "It doesn't change what we must do."

"No," said Caitlyn. "A regrettable waste of talent."

Stone's heart pounded. They were going to kill him. His mind grasped at sounds. Where was the nearest soldier? Could he wrest a rifle from one and gun down Bale and the others before the other soldiers finished him?

Stall. Distract. "Congrats," he said to Bale. "You passed the test."

"Test?"

"Every pack of colonists resisting the UN have been amateurs. I had to prove to myself that you were professionals. You are. I still haven't figured out how you detected me observing you just now."

"And we haven't figured out how you found this location." Bale grinned. "Answer me that and I'll return the favor."

Would answering Bale reveal any of the UN's capabilities it would need to fight the Minervans? No. Bale had already taken his toolkit and his men would bring in the invisibility cloak and the parasail pieces soon enough.

"I accessed public records and found the paper trail of High Emprise LLC. I hitched a ride on your trailer to enter the warehouse complex on the south side of Euler City. My flash bang grenade—"

"I'd surmised."

"I climbed to the roof, observed your...."

Who stalled whom? In twenty minutes the tugs would detach the wormhole. The hundred and fifty plague vector drones would traverse to Earth maybe ten minutes after that.

The soldier at Stone's four o'clock breathed slower than the others and shifted his weight more. Eight or ten feet. Could he do it?

"...drone fleet, parasailed off the roof. I assumed your men brought the drones out here, so I put a tracker on the trailer, then came out here by car to the wormhole site and on foot the rest of the way." With his hands staying on his head, Stone pivoted his elbows from the sides to the front, both to keep his arms limber and to accustom the soldiers to believe his motions remained harmless. To Bale, he said, "Your turn."

"My turn?"

Before Stone replied, Sheila van Bentum emerged from the canopy. She wore the same style of hat as Caitlyn and it looked out of place on a priestess of the Minervans' state non-religion.

What was she doing here? Blessing of the death drones?

Shriving the sins of the captured spy before his execution?

"You agreed to tell me how you detected me just now."

Bale chuckled, a cold sound in the warm morning. "I shan't play 'before I kill you, Mr. Bond.'"

Stone's mouth turned arid. "You swear to me you can save the world and you expect me to take your ability to do so at face value? Dammit, you're amateurs after all." His gaze darted to Caitlyn. "Now's the time."

"Time?"

"To get me the hell out of this."

She laughed, like a Valkyrie might at a mortal man. "You haven't figured it out? Stone, I almost killed you in Kovar's empty garage on Freeland. I almost killed you in your sleep in the pilot's stateroom in *Lady Lux*. I would have killed you within minutes of your arrival at the UN tower if I hadn't realized what the Minervans offered us." She lifted her chin. Her hazel eyes regarded him with a trace of sadness. "We consecrated you. You had your chance to live in alignment with the univ—"

Stone lunged toward the soldier at his four o'clock. Two sprinting strides. He grabbed the rifle before the soldier responded. Swung up, wrenching the rifle from the soldier's grip, clocking the soldier under the chin.

He pivoted. Moved the barrel handguard to his left hand, the trigger to his right. Like women's bodies, each unique in a thousand subtle ways, but all conforming to the same template. Safety off. Raise the sights to his eye. Sunglasses and trimmed brown beard. Squeeze the trigger.

The trigger didn't budge.

He pulled the trigger even harder.

Nothing.

Jammed. Dammit. His left hand worked the charging lever. Brass flicked out of the chamber. Another round snapped home. He aimed again at Bale.

The trigger still refused to move.

What the hell? A setup—

Pine branches and blue sky wheeled across his vision. His back slammed hard ground. A line across his calf muscles throbbed.

The soldier he'd disarmed had swept his legs—

He looked up at a semicircle of rifle muzzles aimed at his chest. The unit leader's wide-set green eyes regarded him impassively. "Our weapons are biometrically and cryptographically locked to the individual soldier."

Stone laid the rifle on the ground and caught his breath. He'd faced death before, but never this close. If even one moment remained, he had a chance.

"Here?" the unit leader said.

"Good as anywhere," Bale's voice replied.

The unit leader nodded. "Ready."

Adrenaline drove Stone's elbows into the ground for leverage, pawed his heels for purchase. His shoes sent pebbles skittering.

"Aim."

No—

Sheila van Bentum's husky voice cried, "Convocation!"

CHAPTER 16

A crown of hot pain ringed Stone's head.

Delight bubbled up his chest. He lived. He would take any amount of pain over oblivion.

Why hadn't the soldiers shot him yet? And what the hell was convocation?

He levered himself onto his left elbow… and the ring of pain around his head tightened. His upper body collapsed to the ground.

Agony squeezed his skull, his brain, his mind. Under the pressure, emotions long unfelt, memories long buried, jetted into his consciousness. Guilt, shame, hate, love, joy, tagged with times and places. People he'd wronged. People he'd done right. The emotions flowed over his consciousness like viscous liquids spilled on a smooth table, then dribbled off the sides, into his body.

His face contorted, eyes twitching, mouth lopsided and pulled open. His limbs trembled. Nausea clenched his stomach.

Stone gasped breaths. His limbs flailed, pounded the dusty ground. Sweat drenched his clothes and trickled down his temples and neck. Inchoate noises burbled from his mouth. His eyes misted at the memories of unnecessary killings and lies that lured women into his bed. A warm nodule in his chest reminded him of the few good things he'd done, coaching boys in football, accompanying his mother when she needed an escort to her charity events. Then his eyes cleared and the warm nodule vanished. *You never asked dad to get therapy for alcoholism* lashed him with guilt, then blew away in the emotional gale.

The pain around his head transmuted into a snug presence seemingly gluing him to the ground. Through the storm of emotions he sensed the hot, sun-dappled clearing; Caitlyn, Bale, and Sheila van Bentum standing together sharing expectant looks; the soldiers shifting their weight and letting their rifle muzzles drift away from Stone's chest; a faint roar somewhere in the western sky. His perceptions were amplified, as if he heard through high-gain microphones and saw through an immense telescope at maximum magnification, yet at the same time the people around him seemed infinitely distant.

"Why isn't the facilitatrix doing something?" muttered one soldier. His shoulder-slung rifle pointed skyward.

"A woman is never supposed to facilitate a man's convocation," replied another, muzzle aimed at the ground.

"But she's the only facili—"

"Quiet," came the unit leader's low, crisp voice. His green eyes cast a sharp glance at his two subordinates.

The emotional storm subsided to a gale. Stone's muscles relaxed. His face unwound its contortions. The torrent of emotions drained, leaving shards of memories like the clutter of leaves and branches and garbage left behind when floodwaters receded. He still couldn't move. If only he could run—

A black rectangle ringed with a thin gray bezel appeared in the center of his vision, like a computer monitor in Gray's office overlaid against the cloudless blue sky. Bright red words in the middle read *Convocation complete.*

Convocation. Obviously the soldiers knew what it meant. In his hotel room half a day ago, Stone had learned Sheila facilitated Gerald Berglund's daughter through it. A ritual Minervans underwent in a Center around their eighteenth birthday. But what the hell had he gained by undergoing it?

What had Caitlyn and the others gained by subjecting him to it?

The red words scrolled to the top of the window. New ones appeared in the center.

Rolston Gridley Wentworth "Stone" Chalmers
Public-facing profile (algorithm: esb-2078.34.113;
block: 6814044)

———

Adventurous, courageous, and extremely cynical.

Spy and assassin employed by [United Nations Interagency Coordination Authority]/[UNICA].

He kills with minimal conscience. His killings are excused by his employment. Persons he has killed include [Paul Ulrich], [Teresa Benavides] <remainder of list omitted for brevity, [fullest known list] accessible>. He has negligible interest in political justifications for his actions.

He also seduces with minimal conscience. Sexual encounters include [Teresa Benavides], [Melanie (surname unknown)], [Annika Kim] <remainder of list omitted for brevity, [fullest known list] accessible>. Sexual encounter with [Melanie (surname unknown)] involved mutual alcohol-impaired consent.

In professional settings, others consider him "highly skilled" and "sexist."

Insufficient information regarding how others consider him in social settings.

[Detailed profile] and [consecration profile] accessible.

Reputation score: 4

The words hung over him while he caught his breath. Public-facing profile? What did that mean?

How did these words appear in his vision? Had the Minervans hacked his implantable? Fed signals to the fine mesh of transcranial magnetic stim leads woven around his hair follicles?

He could move now. He propped himself on one elbow. Damn, the morning had grown bright. He squinted, shaded his eyes with his free hand. Looked around.

His gaze landed on the unit leader. A black window appeared to the side above the soldier's head.

> *g3kexQM4Tm (pseudonym <Minerva Security Directorate*
>   *request>*
> *<validation: reputation scores: 5x1000>)*
> *Public-facing profile (algorithm: esb-msd-2081.88.37;*
> *block: 6814044)*

———

> *Sergeant in [Minerva Security Directorate]/[MSD]*
> *[Ground Force]. Training score 98/100. Training completed*
> *2132-04-27. Operations score 97/100. Full compliance with*
> *[Minerva Code of Military Justice] smart contract.*
>
> *Civilians encountering him during course of his duties*
> *consider him "respectful," "disciplined," "a man any*
> *enemies should fear."*
>
> *[Detailed profile] and [consecration profile] accessible.*
>
> *Reputation score: 204*

Stone sat up. Looked around. Black windows appeared near the other soldiers. Corporals and one private, all pseudonymous at MSD request. They scored below their leader, had one or two minor violations of the military justice smart contract, and civilians found them less praiseworthy.

Enough of them. He peered at Bale.

> *Simon Bale*
> *Public-facing profile (algorithm: narrat-2107-11-03;*
> *block: 6814044)*

————

> *Simon Bale is the [High Councillor] of the [Minerva*
> *Security Directorate], holding office since 31st January*
> *2126. Prior to his current office, he worked as a senior*
> *investigator for the [Euler City Police Department] and*
> *deputy commander of the [MSD Colonial Police]. The*
> *[MSDCP] foiled an attempted 51% attack on the [Center for*
> *Alignment with the Universe] convocation blockchain*
> *during his tenure. His leadership is considered by*
> *knowledgable persons of high reputation <[link]> to have*
> *been a key determinant of [MSDCP]'s success.*

> *Bale is highly reputed <[link]> to be honest, diligent,*
> *patriotic, and pious. He is married with three sons....*

Stone skimmed the rest. The profile omitted "plotter of genocidal pandemic." Which meant all the data forced into Stone's vision was a lie.

Right?

He rose on wobbly legs. The soldiers brought their muzzles halfway to Stone's chest. He looked past them, to Bale, Sheila, and Caitlyn. "What—" His voice seized up like an unoiled gearbox. He cleared his throat. "What have you done? How? Why?"

Caitlyn raised slender fingers toward the two Minervans. "I should be the one to explain. This is part of your culture. Stone wasn't raised to expect this. Just like me."

She came closer. A black window opened over her shoulder.

Caitlyn Fredriksen
Public-facing profile—

Stone swiped his left hand at air. He knew her already. The black window vanished. So did the others. The way they disappeared told him he could reopen any of them with a thought.

The soldiers parted for her. She stopped six feet from Stone. Her hazel eyes glittered like onyx. "Stone, you've put it together, haven't you? I've worked to save Earth from its corrupt and incompetent government since before we met."

"You and who else?" She might slip some intel. How the hell to get it to Gray he'd figure out later.

She dismissed the question with an arched eyebrow. "I've worked to forge alliances with colonial forces that could help us achieve our goal. On Freeland, we thought the Benavides family could lead a guerrilla war against the UN, which would erode popular support on Earth for UN peacekeeping policies. Not a killing blow, but the first slash in a death of a thousand cuts."

"You only joined forces with me because your attack dogs slipped the leash."

"Teresa Benavides' plan to destroy the wormhole, if successful, would have ruined all sympathy for the Freelanders among the average person on Earth. She had to be stopped. Your interest and mine aligned at that point."

Stone sniffed out a breath. "You seriously thought fifty thousand Freelanders could resist Earth?"

"We had to play the hand dealt to us."

He thought of their joint mission. "You didn't try to turn Ulrich's people into a guerrilla force."

"On Trinity," she said, "we thought whoever stole the interplanetary ship plans would wish to use *Lady Lux*, the missing warpdrive ship, to flee somewhere outside the UN's jurisdiction and start a new colony. Given decades to build up a technological and industrial base, during decades when Earth's decline would steepen, a new colony could resist Earth and eventually fight back."

"If you wanted Ulrich and the others to lead their followers on a ten thousand light year exodus, you never told them that."

"My plan was to strangle you in your sleep," Caitlyn said, "then tell them everything. I would have had to join them on their trek and never return to Earth. Not ideal, but a price I would have paid. Then Laclede invaded our cabin with the only firearm on *Lady Lux* and, well, you know the rest."

Stone's gaze flicked over the camouflaged soldiers and Bale's hardened face. "The scout ship report on Minerva made you think they had the technological and industrial base to fight back."

"The report was promising enough to bring me out here with the diplomatic mission," Caitlyn said. "But when I discovered what the Centers did, and how they did it, I saw a chance to free Earth from the UN without an interstellar war."

"If ships and soldiers can't bring down the UN, how the hell can—" He touched his aching forehead. He expected a mushy strip of softened bone, but his fingers found throbbing muscle and warmth like hot wires under his skin. "—convocation do it?"

"As the Minervans say, consecration allows you to truly know yourself. Convocation allows everyone to truly know everyone else."

Stone pictured himself strolling down Lexington Avenue. Every pedestrian on the sidewalk reading the open book of his public profile and cringing.

Not just because they saw his secrets. Because they knew he saw theirs.

Bah. His public profile revealed things he'd rather hide? A simple fix: edit it. Just like everyone else would. He lived in Manhattan, where everyone cultivated a public persona and kept their true selves hidden. He nodded toward Bale and Sheila. "You believe them?"

"I'll tell you how the Minervans do it, and you'll realize why I believe them and why you should too."

"I'm listening." Not just to her. The wormhole tugs' engines rumbled like far-off thunder. How could he stop them from launching the drones?

A glance found Bradley dell'Angelo seated under the canopy. His slack face showed his attention lay on data projected to his sensory nerves. Get past the soldiers, get past Caitlyn and Bale, kill dell'Angelo with bare hands before he launched the drones....

"Decades ago the Minervans developed brain/computer interfaces. Like the transcranial magnetic stimulator wiring we have, but better. They use medical nanotechnology to grow a quantum computer within our skull bones and to wire that computer into many parts of the brain. Their wiring even accesses the subconscious and the emotions. Convocation requires that access."

Stone touched his forehead again. "My head hurts because your nanomachines grew a computer inside my skull."

"Nanomachines did that, but they didn't cause your headache." She grinned. "I'll get to that soon."

"Get to it now."

"Aren't you curious how those nanomachines entered your skull?"

Stone's brow creased. Two evenings ago with Sheila in the Center, part of consecration? He remembered a fingerprick. To draw blood for DNA profiling, he'd assumed, but had they injected him with nanomachines then?

He rubbed his forehead. His head hurt worse than it had from that sinus headache his first morning in the UN tower....

A dry swallow, then he said, "You aerosolized the nanomachines."

"Not me," Caitlyn said. "You found the name Matthew Thomas, I take it?"

The UN tower... Despite the warm morning, a chill ran down his legs. "You infected everyone who came dirtside from *Yassir Arafat*?"

"Yes. It's dormant for everyone. Except you."

His eyes widened. His gaze swung to the parked trailer, then up the far ridge. Under the shade of the trees, sky blue points swathed in gossamer dotted the pine straw.

"You aren't unleashing a plague on Earth," Stone said. "You're unleashing convocation."

A nod dipped the brim of Caitlyn's broad hat. "Each of the drones carries enough aerosolized nanomachines to wire the brains of—" She turned her hazel eyes to Bale and Sheila. "—ten thousand people?"

Bale spoke. "They'll average twelve thousand, says Dr. Thomas."

Stone did the math in his head. "You'll infect a million and a half people." Then he chuckled. He might not need to kill dell'Angelo after all. "It won't work, keyhole kop."

"Based on my briefing, Bradley dell'Angelo's team targeted the drones to key locations—"

"Not that. You put a computer in my head that learned all my deep dark secrets and broadcasts them to the world. All I have to do is edit what it broadcasts."

Caitlyn laughed like tinkling crystal. "We've come to why you should believe the Minervans can free Earth from the UN."

"Which is?"

"Because your public profile is impossible to edit." Her cheeks tightened. "I'm sure you never heard of blockchain."

"Oh but I have. Watch out for those 51% attacks. They're a doozy."

"You did read High Councillor Bale's public profile." A chuckle flavored the words, then dried up. "Be serious."

He vented tension from his shoulders. The UN would survive the drones reaching Earth. Playing along with her gave him more time to plan his escape. "Enlighten me."

"I hadn't heard of blockchain either before I made contact with Sheila and Simon Bale. The concept arose a century ago but the UN suppressed it before I was born. Maybe even before you were." A teasing smile revealed straight white teeth.

"Skip the cheap shots."

"Blockchain is basically distributed record keeping. Instead of, say, a bank keeping the only ledger of who owes how much money to whom, all the debtors and creditors keep a copy of the ledger and peri-odically update it. Blockchain has some drawbacks. One is that at the time of convocation, your computer downloads the entire existing blockchain. Even with data compression and exponential decay of transactions of deceased people, we're still talking about petabytes of data in a couple of minutes. Even quantum computers handling that workload generate noticeable waste heat."

"That's a hell of a drawback."

"Blockchain has one huge advantage over a bank that outweighs all the drawbacks."

Stone winced and rubbed his forehead. "It better be huge."

"A banker can falsify a ledger. A blockchain can only be falsified if a majority of its ledgers are falsified at the same time. The 51% attack you read about but didn't understand."

"What do financial ledgers have to do with...." Stone's hands juggled air.

"The convocation blockchain is a ledger of reputation," Caitlyn said. To the side, Sheila van Bentum smiled like a stained glass saint.

"Ledger of reputation.... Like customer reviews on the worldweb? Like gossip?" A breeze rustled pine branches. The engines of the wormhole tugs roared a little louder.

"And more," Caitlyn said. "The computer in the skull picks up memories you associate with guilt, shame, embarrassment, and the like. Memories of the wrongs you know you've committed. And memories of your actions that violate social norms. Those too are added to the ledger."

Gooseflesh stippled Stone's cheeks. The drones still posed a risk to the UN. He would still have to break dell'Angelo's neck.

Stone squinted up at the descending wormhole tugs. Blue-white exhaust plumes knifed across the sky. In formation between the tugs, a night sky from Earth showed as a black dot.

Caitlyn said, "You see what the convocation blockchain can do."

"You're going to infect a million and a half key people on Earth. When you activate convocation, they'll broadcast all their secrets. To everyone?"

"No. Only to everyone else who's undergone convocation."

Stone sloughed out a breath. "Then it still won't do what you hope. The UN's high and mighty already know each other's dirty secrets. A web of blackmail makes the world go around."

"Mutual blackmail only works if everyone agrees to play that game. If one person comes clean to the public, the game is over. We think the drones can spread the nanomachines widely enough to reveal the insiders' transgressions to everyone in the settled galaxy."

"You *think*."

She shared a glance with Bale. He flicked an icy gaze to Stone, then nodded.

Caitlyn nodded in reply, then said to Stone, "Nothing is certain, but we can increase our chances."

"How?"

"You can join us."

The soldiers in unison moved their rifles to ready positions, firing finger on the outside of the trigger guard, other hand on the barrel handguard.

"Or," Caitlyn said, "you can die."

CHAPTER 17

"Sign me up!" Stone said.

Neither the soldiers nor their leaders near the canopy moved. On the far slope, men spoke indistinctly to one another and rustled through undergrowth and pine straw. A bird tweeted somewhere amid the pines. Then Bale barked out a laugh.

"It won't be like when you 'joined' us after consecration," Caitlyn said, fingers air-quoting.

"Because I mean it this time. You convinced me."

"*They* convinced you." She gestured at the soldiers ringing Stone.

"We're quibbling."

"You're right. Because if you join us, even if you intend to play double agent, you will be bound to us."

Stone said, "I'm not usually into kink, but when I am, I do the binding."

Caitlyn's face turned humorless. "Do you have one of the soldier's public profiles open?"

"No."

"You figured out how to close them on your own. Good. Open one. Doesn't matter which."

Stone found the green-eyed leader, still the only one with face exposed. An intention to open the man's public profile formed in Stone's mind before he could put into words. The profile reopened. His gaze went to the gobbledygook pseudonym, the validation entry about reputation scores....

"Sheila and the other founders of the blockchain understood that secrecy is at times required. Now that Minerva needs soldiers, for example, their identities need not be exposed to any enemy that might access the blockchain. Accordingly, the founders set up mechanisms to allow agencies that need secrecy to request pseudonymous transaction logging, time-limited gray blockchains, or both for personnel who need it."

More jargon, but one thing stuck out. "Request? So instead of a banker who can forge a ledger, you have a judge who can issue a secret warrant."

"The request is to a set of decentralized, highly-reputable people selected by a—what do you call it, Sheila?"

"A Venetian election," the Minervan woman said. Her eyes crinkled at him. "Stone has too much on his hands for me to pile the details on him."

"I would ignore them anyway," Stone said.

"We know," Caitlyn said. "And there are checks and balances to reduce the risk of abuse." She waved her hand as if wiping away the details. "Our organization—High Emprise LLC and Friends— requested a gray blockchain and smart contract terminating ten years after—" She pointed over her shoulder, to where the tugs' fusion drives threw the shadows of pines over Stone and the others. Only minutes to go. "—placement of the wormhole."

"Meaning?"

"Now, the things we do are shared solely among ourselves. After ten years, they will enter the full blockchain."

"I take it you just described a gray blockchain," Stone said. "What the hell's a smart contract?" A sinking feeling in his gut hinted at the answer.

"A contract implemented by a blockchain. A breach of contract is immediately alert every other party to the contract." She raised her chin. Her hazel eyes peered down her nose from under her broad-brimmed hat. "If you join us, you must enter into a smart contract. Divulging the existence of High Emprise LLC and Friends or any information about our private club's goals or actions to anyone not connected to the full blockchain will be punishable by—?" She looked to Bale and Sheila.

Bale turned frosty blue eyes on Stone. He enunciated his next word. "Death."

Sheila winced. "I wish I didn't...." Her husky voice trailed off.

"You do," Bale said.

"Yes. When I joined you, I knew I might have to grasp the nettle. I agree with the High Councillor. Death."

Caitlyn glanced down and to her left. "Matthew and Bradley agree."

Under the canopy, Bradley dell'Angelo lifted a hand in their direction, while his gaze drilled into a sight only he could see.

Caitlyn looked at Stone with eyes like onyx. "I agree too. And before you think you've found a loophole, yes, by the terms of the contract, you may divulge the existence of our private club to people who are connected to the full blockchain. But divulging the name of any member, or our goals, or actions, to anyone will also be punishable by death."

Bale grunted. "If you attempt sabotage, death." His blue eyes peered at Stone. "You're not the type to sacrifice yourself, but if you were, and after revealing our secrets tried to cover your tracks by suicide, your embedded quantum computer stores enough power to transmit your treachery to us."

"You're right that I'm not the type."

The blue eyes turned icy. "Don't waste your breath telling us what we already know."

Death if he didn't join them. Death if he joined and double-crossed them.

But death how? Could the quantum computer in his skull destroy his brain? Or did *death* only mean a death sentence, to be carried out by.... His gaze took in the soldiers, the unit leader, Bale. Caitlyn.

If he could slip away from them, then fight his executioner when he —or she—hunted him, he liked his chances.

Stone lifted his chest. "I understand what I'm getting into. Sign me up."

Caitlyn bowed her head to Sheila van Bentum. "Facilitatrix?"

"You don't need me to bless his entry into our, what did you call it, private club," replied the Minervan woman in her husky voice.

"I don't. He doesn't. But…." Caitlyn nodded at the soldiers, looked up and down the group of workmen scattered through the forest. "Many others do."

Sheila stepped forward. Despite wearing khaki outdoors wear instead of her red dress embedding a constellation of diamonds, she bore herself like a priestess. The soldiers stepped back for her and bowed their heads. Even Bale dipped his chin.

"Stone Chalmers, do you knowingly choose to join High Emprise LLC and Friends, to further its goals, to settle all conflicts of interest in its favor, and to keep its secrets for the duration of the contract, with any breach by you of this contract punishable by your death?"

His heart thumped like a gong. "Yes."

A trickle of warmth ringed his head. On flexed knees and with held breath, he braced for emotional impact.

Nothing.

Stone exhaled, inhaled. Looked around. Thought open the private profile windows for every member of High Emprise LLC and Friends in and around the clearing. The same black rectangles appeared over each shoulder, but now their bezels were thick bands of deep red, pulsing like a heartbeat. In the bezel above each window hung crisp white lettering.

Private Blockchain - High Emprise LLC and Friends - Private Blockchain

The soldiers' private profiles indicated the men all tested high for genetic and personality markers of loyalty and secrecy. The Minerva Security Directorate had assembled this unit solely to assign it to High Emprise. The men were all Level 2 members with 0% voting rights.

A glance around the clearing showed the other security guards at Level 1, and the workmen at Level 0. Security clearances? Likely: Bale and Sheila held Level 4 membership and 18% voting rights each.

Caitlyn—

A chill ran down Stone's bare limbs.

> *Caitlyn Fredriksen*
> *Level 3 member*
> *10% voting right*

> *Recruited by her mentor, [Robert Holbrook] of [United*
> *Nations Interstellar Transport Bureau], to overthrow the*
> *UN, she contacted High Councillor [Bale] and Facilitatrix*
> *[van Bentum] 2131-12-29. After undergoing consecration*
> *2132-01-03 and convocation 2132-01-06, she joined High*
> *Emprise LLC and Friends 2132-02-09 in planning [Operation*
> *Sunlight]—*

Stone blinked. Holbrook wielded great power. He had to relay this intel to Gray. But how?

Caitlyn's profile shrank down to a tab at the bottom of the rectangle. New text took its place.

Operation Sunlight

Ah, by blinking he'd clicked on a hyperlink in brackets.

He read more.

> *Motto: Sunlight is the best disinfectant.*
> *Drones will be dispatched to Earth. The drones will bear*
> *medical-grade nanomachines configured to construct*
> *quantum computers—*

He knew all that. He skimmed, clicked on *Next Page,* and skimmed more.

> *—targets include:*
> *Secretary-General Abdullah Sayyid*
> *Fatimah Sayyid*
> *UNICA Director Karlheinz Kroebel*
> *Luise Kroebel*
> *UNICA Assistant Director of Operational Planning*
> *Martindale Gray*
> *UNITB Assistant Director of Security Robert Holbrook—*

Gray actually was the old man's surname. Widowed, divorced, or never married? From Gray's mentions of grandchildren, probably never married and throwing a smoke screen.

Stone squeezed shut his eyes, not believing the next line. Yet when he reopened them, he still read Holbrook on the list of targets. Why had Caitlyn chosen to target him?

The list continued. Pages of *UN Ambassador from;* US President Kwame Goldbaum and the prime ministers of twenty European and Far Eastern countries, plus their domestic political rivals; administrators and faculty members at fifty universities; the CEOs of the Global-Fortune 500; a hundred influential pundits on the worldforum; a hundred prosecutors and law enforcement officials.

And their spouses. Perhaps that was High Emprise's plan. All the wives and the few husbands at the highest social stratum who were ignorant of how their spouses amassed wealth and power—or pretended to be ignorant—would get the truth shoved in their plastic surgery faces. A dream for gossip bloggers and divorce lawyers.

Not enough to topple the UN.

Still, he had to get this intel to Gray. Somehow.

Stone noticed the Minervans' gazes on him. He thought closed all the windows.

Bale rubbed his beard with his palm. His blue eyes darted over something over Stone's left shoulder. "The new recruit has his first assignment."

"I agree," said Caitlyn.

Sheila opened her palms. "I trust your judgement."

"Me too." Bradley dell'Angelo's soft voice barely emerged from the canopy.

Stone scowled at Caitlyn. "My first assignment?"

"You didn't read your profile?"

"I know my own mind. Now you do too." He spoke with banter.

"We know you composed two reports about our private club to Gray," said Caitlyn flatly. "One is in the safe in your room at the UN tower. The other is in the diplomatic pouch waiting for transport to Earth."

All traces of levity vanished from Stone's face, like water in a gully under the midday Minervan sun. "I subvoked those before I joined you. I can't be in breach of contract for something I did before I signed the contract."

Bale's voice cut the air between them. "We are honorable people. This isn't Earth, Mr. Chalmers."

"What's my assignment?"

"You must retrieve those reports and hand them to Ms. Fredriksen for destruction before the road and rail links to Earth are constructed. If you fail in that task, then you would be in breach."

"I will succeed." Stone didn't need the encrypted sticks to pass intel to Gray. He could read aloud the profiles stored in his node of High Emprise's gray blockchain. "If someone can give me a lift back to the UN tower—"

"Not yet," said Sheila van Bentum. "The roadway and rail line to Earth won't be connected for two days."

Caitlyn stepped closer to Stone. Her hat's brim nearly brushed his cheek. "I've never seen a wormhole placement. Have you?"

"Only from the Earth side."

"Seen one, seen them all, I'm sure. But I haven't seen one and I want to. And I'd like you to join me. Doing so will show your team spirit."

"A team I had to join or else get a rifle round through my brain?" He shrugged. "Sure. I've got nothing else to do."

"Follow me." She strode away from the canopy, up the southern slope of the valley. Her lean legs, smooth and lightly tanned between her shorts and hiking socks, should've allured him, but didn't. Amazing what getting press-ganged by fanatics could do to his mood.

They wound their way past drones lying on the pine straw. Workmen crouched with instruments, running final diagnostics. A bright light from the south doubled the shadows of the trees. Near the crest of the ridge, the pines grew short and twisted, and bare rocks poked through a thin cover of scree and fallen needles.

She reached the top first. "Wow. What a sight."

Visible between pine trunks, The wormhole was a night-black circle half the size of a full moon. It contrasted with the pale blue sky, and the four exhaust plumes of the tugs framed it like a golden setting for a black diamond. The tugs' engines screamed now, a sound that should be inflicted on some poor bastard in Queens, living under the flight path of suborbitals into Kennedy. The wormhole crept down the sky as the tugs holding it by invisible cords matched their descent with their dance partners lowering the Earth end toward the Mojave Desert.

"Could the Minervans have shot down the tugs?" Stone asked. "Or *Yassir Arafat*?"

"I don't know, but I believe so."

"Why didn't they? Ah." He saw the answer before she put it into words.

"*Yassir Arafat* and the tugs are in continual contact through the wormhole with Earth. The Minervans couldn't make it look like an accident. The UN would launch a punitive expedition to slag Minerva back to lifeless rock."

"Minerva might be able to fight them off."

"The UN is still strong enough to break direct resistance. And Minerva is too precious to squander as cannon fodder."

Stone raised an eyebrow. "Precious? How much of their koolaid did you drink?"

"I've been consecrated and joined the convocation almost nine months ago. I'm the most focused and at the same time the calmest I've ever been. And I would be even if the Minervans couldn't help us save the human race."

"Oh, yeah, from that UN tyranny." Sarcasm thickened his words.

The broad-brimmed hat amplified a gentle shake of her head. "Worse. From UN incompetence."

The wormhole's slow descent finally carried it below the tops of the trees on the nearest intervening ridge. The tugs followed the wormhole out of sight ten seconds later. The engine scream filled the air, frightening birds and the small animals of the undergrowth into silence.

"There's a camera feed from the top of a tree about a quarter of a mile away," she said. She pushed a link to him from her implantable through his. After interfacing through the Minervan blockchain quantum computers, using the older Earth tech seemed like writing a letter with pen and paper.

He opened the link. A magnified image filled his mind's eye. Fusion exhaust softened the rocky ground in four spots outside the crater. Harder boulders slumped like empty vape cartridges littered on melting snowpiles. The equilibrator ring around the wormhole's equator shone like a platinum wedding band in dazzling sunlight. The black sphere of the wormhole itself swallowed the daylight.

The bottom of the wormhole dipped below the crater wall. The softened ground melted. Lava like brown and red pus oozed across the ground, rippling under the downforce of the drive exhausts. The tugs descended, engines burning furiously to control the placement of the wormhole's tons of exotic matter in sync with their partners on the Earth side.

Presumably the tug pilots derived great meaning from their work. Or feared the crushing notoriety of failure.

The tugs hung in the air atop pillars of fire for long seconds. Then in a blink they shot upward. Traces of the Tobias Becker persona from Trinity tried estimating the acceleration of their ascent.

Stone shook away the useless thought. The tugs rose because they'd released their cables in unison. "Wormhole in place," he said. A link to a different camera popped up and he subvoked to it. A camera in the road and rail cut in the crater rim, looking downward. The equilibrator ring rested on the crater floor. A hemisphere of desert night rose above it.

Caitlyn stared at the tugs rising through her naked-eye field of view. "I know."

The roar of the tug engines reverberated through the trees around Stone. Another sound joined them, high and faint, as if he strolled through a park along the East River and every weedwhacker in Brooklyn fired up at once.

Stone looked over his shoulder.

A hundred and fifty drones rose from the sun-dappled pine straw and filed between the trees, heading south.

CHAPTER 18

They returned to Euler City in a black coupe Caitlyn summoned from the UN motor pool. The air conditioning reached full power just as the coupe turned off the gravel road onto the paved road slicing through the parallel ridges.

After turning left at the intersection with the main highway, they passed a steady stream of oncoming vehicles, mostly pickup trucks bearing the logos of Minervan construction companies. Workmen heading west to the wormhole site to finish the road and rail lines to Earth.

Even with their advanced tech and a round-the-clock schedule, they would need about forty-eight hours to finish construction. Given the venality and petty ineptitude of Gautam, the mail clerk at the UN tower, Stone could add another dozen hours to the window of time he had to retrieve the report to Gray.

The wormhole's placement impacted the lives of more Minervans than just the construction crews. As they approached downtown Euler City, conversation bubbled under the sunscreens over sidewalk cafés. The locals raised demitasses of espresso and quart steins of beer with warm smiles.

One woman's gaze, brown eyes in a pale face framed by long auburn hair, landed on the coupe's window while it waited for pedestrians to cross the street. Stone sucked in a breath.

"Her quantum computer can't identify you through the window tint," Caitlyn said. She sat next to him on the rear seat, her legs together and crossed at the knee. "That means she can't see your profile on the public blockchain."

"Good." He spoke with forced casualness. "Wouldn't want to scare the locals."

But his embedded quantum computer could identify the woman's. He skipped past her name—not relevant—and found the great shame of her life; at the age of sixteen, one cloudless evening in a riverfront park, she'd let a boy run his hand up her skirt. Since then—

The coupe drove on. The window shrank away before he could read the woman's attempts to redeem herself. Not that she'd done anything wrong in his mind. "The Minervans won't let anyone live down anything, will they?"

"Childhood is private. The quantum computer won't push to the blockchain anything embarrassing, unethical, or illegal you did before age thirteen."

"What's the point? Twelve-year-olds can't get into any real trouble."

Caitlyn raised an eyebrow. "Even you?"

"I wasn't that precocious."

She ignored his comment. "Also, parent-child relationships are private until the child turns eighteen. Same for intimate relationships after the couple gets engaged."

Stone laughed with an edge of nervous disbelief. "Everyone's a virgin until they get married?"

"Pretty much." She shook her head. "Don't worry. Even if everyone on Earth joined the convocation, pre-marital chastity won't become the norm for decades yet."

The windows of the Center for Alignment with the Universe glowed blue, green, and gold in afternoon sunlight. "I thought Operation Sunlight targeted a million people, not five billion."

"That's right." Her hazel eyes betrayed nothing.

Which told him what he needed to know. The voting members of High Emprise LLC and Friends at levels 3 and 4 of the security hierarchy could change the plan without him knowing. At least they'd assigned him to level 2, a notch above the workmen launching drones in the forest, and on par with the soldiers in their advanced camouflage bodysuits.

A red glint from a stained glass facilitatrix' dress caught Stone's eye as the coupe drove past. A question came to mind. "If you have a plan that doesn't need me, why did you bring me into your conspiracy?"

She nodded. "As soon as I identified you among the arrivals from *Yassir Arafat*, Bale argued for killing you. Sheila and I believed you might be more useful to us alive than dead."

"I have that effect on women." Stone smirked. "Especially two at once."

Caitlyn rolled her eyes. "You and I have at least one thing in common."

"Oh?"

"Like you told me on the flight to the Trinity wormhole, I too don't shit where I eat." She went on. "Sheila's argument was that we needed a test subject to confirm that unfacilitated convocation could work. In my view, setting aside your many flaws, you are effective at tradecraft. Even though we thought we could win enough tricks to make our bid, recruiting you was drawing an ace in the hole."

"Are you playing bridge or poker?"

"I'm mixing metaphors?" She gave a tinkling laugh. "Bridge, then. We aren't bluffing."

Stone eased back in the seat. They passed the Minervan government buildings in silence. The coupe turned left, onto a boulevard with only a guardrail between their travel lanes and the bluff overlooking the Wisdom Sea. The crash of waves reached them from the shore below as the UN tower loomed in the distance.

Minutes later they reached the tower. The coupe rolled into the parking garage entrance. The entry gate lifted and the coupe pulled into the nearest gap in the row of parked vehicles. Behind plexiglass windows in the motor pool office, cups of cold coffee rested on a desk strewn with smartpaper. Lifts held an orange sedan man-high above the concrete floor of the maintenance bay. Stone climbed out. Caitlyn handed him his toolkit and the 9mm pistols.

As they crossed to the elevator, their footsteps echoed in the empty space. "Where is everyone?" Caitlyn asked.

"Wormhole party."

"At 1400?"

"Any excuse to start drinking. For half of them, their mission is over and they're attitude is screw-it-got-my-orders."

Caitlyn's lips mashed together.

"Weren't you the one," Stone said, "who told me UN employees are corrupt and incompetent?"

She forced a chuckle. "The reality of it still surprises me. It doesn't surprise you?"

They neared the elevators. Stone arched an eyebrow and subvoked *Up.* "No."

She switched to subvocal through their embedded quantum computers. [Yet you still hold back from believing in us. Don't lie.] The elevator car hummed down the shaft toward them. [I know you signed the smart contract to avoid getting shot. I'm sure you're scheming about how to report us to Gray.]

The elevator opened. Stone gestured for her to enter. He gazed at the blond locks flowing down her graceful neck. How easy to snap it…

…and how easy for the soldiers to hunt him down?

He followed her in. [What's your point?]

The doors slid together. [You know how corrupt and inept the UN is. Why fight for it?]

To the elevator, he said, "Eighty." To Caitlyn, he rolled his eyes. [Because your Minervan friends are equally incompetent. What, you think they know what they're doing?]

The elevator zoomed upward. She pinched her nose and exhaled. [They have the cohesion of a group of founders, and the blockchain to maintain their cohesion. So, yes.]

Stone worked his jaw against the pressure of the rising elevator.

The car slowed and stopped at his floor. Music and the chatter of a crowd trickled down from the top of the shaft.

[Almost everyone will be partying in the penthouse,] he said.

[Good. That will make it easier to get the second encrypted stick.] She nodded out the open elevator doors. [Now we get the first.]

He led the way around the corner and down the long hallway leading to his suite. The door opened for him. After the dark hallway, daylight glared through open blinds. He strode in and beckoned her to follow. Her footsteps padded into the suite and the door swung closed with a whisper from the hinges and a quiet thud.

The safe opened for his thumbprint and retina. He reached in for the stick with last night's message to Gray. Tossed it to Caitlyn with an easy underhand motion.

She plucked it from the air and shoved it in a pocket of her cargo shorts. "We're done here."

One hand on the safe door, Stone put on a lazy grin. "What about the other stick?"

"The one you wrote as part of the Lavallette cover story? I don't need it." She gave a knowing smile in return, then turned as a motion in khaki for the door.

"Wait." He gestured at his jogging clothes, then hooked his thumb toward the bathroom. "I'm going to change. You should to."

She faced him, palm on her hipbone. "Why?"

"Everyone else will be in desk jockey clothes until they change to party wear. We'll look out of place. Like we spent last night and all of today outdoors."

Caitlyn weighed his words, then said, "Good call."

"You're still quartered with the diplomatic mission holdovers?"

"The Minervans moved us all to rooms here in the tower. Sometime yesterday. I'm on 37, apparently."

"I'll come by with the stick from the diplomatic pouch."

She shook her head. "I'll meet you back here and we'll head down together. Understood?"

"You do outrank me."

A moment later, she left. Stone went into the suite's bedroom. A spritz of cologne and a change of clothes? Wait, he was waiting for a woman to get dressed. Forget the French bath; he had time for soap and hot water.

While he showered, he searched for the current location of Gautam the mail clerk. Upstairs, probably drinking, certainly far away from the transparent floor hanging over the crater rim. Stone wondered if Merrill had found out how low Gautam ranked and moved on, then filed the irrelevant thought. The communication office was empty.

Who else worked on the third floor? His implantable found offices, found names, searched for locations. Most everyone was upstairs, except for one woman in her room on the sixtieth floor. Even better. No one would see him and Caitlyn sneaking around the communication office.

He cut the water, toweled off, dressed in a V-neck shirt and tight pants. After he retrieved the encrypted stick, he would join the party. Drunk women giddy in the afterglow of the wormhole placement. Fish, barrel, and one of his last times on the treadmill before Caitlyn tried to play him as an ace card—

Knuckles tapped the door. He opened it to find Caitlyn in a red blouse and a skirt with a beaded hem. Bare toes and sandal straps peeked under her skirt.

[You're casual,] he said through his embedded quantum computer.

[Playing the part. Ready?]

Stone slipped into canvas loafers and slung the toolkit over one shoulder. He pulled the door shut. After the latch clicked closed, he led her to the elevator.

As they descended, she asked, [Can you cut off security camera feeds in the hallway?]

[Don't need to. I invoked Protocol Eleven-J on tower security.]

The elevator slowed. The doors opened with a ping. No trace of sound from the party a thousand feet above. Stone headed out of the elevator and rounded the corner toward the communication office.

He stopped in front of the office's closed door. Pulled a scanner from his toolkit. Cameras in the hallway didn't worry him, but sensors on the door did. If Gautam had rigged the door to alert him if someone went into the office wanting to add something to the diplomatic pouch, he might barge in and force Stone to kill him.

Imagine the paperwork.

Stone ran the scanner along the door frame.

[What's that?] asked Caitlyn.

The scanner's electromagnetic field strength display hovered around zero. [You ever do any breaking and entering on the job?]

[I'm trained.]

He passed the scanner over the top corner of the door above the handle. [Just say *no*.] The needle in the display bounced up. He continued the sweep. No other items. Just a pair of proximity sensors, one on the door and the other on the frame, forming a circuit that would alert when broken.

Stone tapped the scanner's display, called up the *mimic* function, and held the scanner up to the corner of the door. [Open it. Go in.]

Caitlyn did. He followed her, sliding the scanner over the frame as he went. On the inside, the sensor on the frame showed a round black bump.

[Close the door.]

She eased the door shut. A telltale on the scanner showed the sensor on the door closed the circuit. He pulled the scanner down, turned it off.

The waiting room looked as shabby as it had the previous morning. In the video loop, a high tide isolated Mont-Saint-Michel. The closed window in the opaque glass wall shielded the workroom from view.

Beside the window in the corner of the room, a door of the same milky glass stood flush against the opaque wall. One handle, one deadbolt, both with key locks.

Pick the locks later. He scanned again. Two alarm circuits this time, one formed of prox sensors like the front door, another a motion sensor. From the scanner signal, it looked like the motion sensor's beam formed one side of a triangle, with the glass wall forming another and the grown bone side wall of the office forming a third.

Stone smiled to himself. Easy. [Same door as the first one, but after you go in, step over the motion sensor cutting the corner.] He pointed at the glass wall on the outside of where the motion sensor stood, then bent his arm to indicate the beam path.

She nodded.

He picked the locks, foiled the door's prox sensors, then lifted the handle. He high-stepped over the motion sensor beam into the workroom.

Easy so far, but if he failed to find the encrypted stick, Caitlyn would still try to kill him.

CHAPTER 19

Blinds on the far wall smothered Minervan sunlight. A tang laced the air from the glue gun mounted on its telescoping arm near the front glass wall. Plastic shelves neatly arrayed with office supplies jutted from the bone wall on the right. A thin plastic desk in the corner. A dozen black boxes about one foot by one by two long, stacked three-high along the wall to the left, each sealed with a round UN logo sticker.

Stone switched the handheld scanner to RFID reader mode and crossed the room's tan carpet.

[There's a diplomatic pouch in each box?] Caitlyn asked.

[The box is the pouch]. He scanned the first. *UN mission, UNITBS Yassir Arafat*, dated three months earlier.

[Ah. The term must date back a few centuries. They used to send messages written on paper in a bag or pouch.]

Stone went to the other end. Knelt. Scanned the top box. *UN mission, Euler City, Minerva.* Today's date.

Second box in the stack. Dated yesterday.

A grin pushed up the corners of his mouth. He set aside the top box of the stack. Lifted yesterday's. Put it on the floor in front of him. With his gaze on the UN sticker on the lid and sidewall, he reached into his toolkit for a small knife. [I need another sticker.]

[Where? —I see a carton.] Caitlyn padded on her sandals to the shelves on the far wall. The carton of security stickers stood next to some antiques for handling paper mail: a block of wax, a seal, a set of letter openers.

He sliced through the sticker. Even if she couldn't find one to cover his tracks, he still had to get the encrypted stick out of the box. On discovering a compromised sticker, Gautam would just scrape it off and slap a new one on. The time and date stamp generated when the sticker unpeeled from its backing would differ from the date code readable from the box' RFID chip, but the mail clerk would hope none of his superiors would notice.

Stone sniffed out a chuckle. His superiors were UN flunkies too. If they noticed a discrepancy, they would bury it and hope *their* superiors never found out.

A sobering thought trickled down his chest. A Minervan would never do that.

He inhaled and pushed out a breath. Refocused, he opened the lid. Scores of memory sticks jumbled together, a riot of garish colors like the bin of toy cars his father had been too busy to play with in Stone's childhood.

Another focusing breath. Dump the box of memory sticks. Ping the one he needed through his implantable. In the middle of the pile.

Stone spread the sticks on the carpet. A red stripe. Three blue bumps. No, four; Gautam had added an RFID address label. There— no, two red lines, not one stripe. Was that—? Only one bump. There? Maroon, not crimson.

There. Right color, right width. Stone ran his fingertips over the red stripe. Four bumps. One bump uneven from excess glue. He pinged it through his implantable to make sure. He didn't recognize the sender's name, but he'd burned the destination address into his memory four months earlier.

[Here you go.] he said. Caitlyn, one hand behind her back, watched him with her hazel eyes. He tossed her the stick.

She slipped it into a pocket hidden in her skirt, then grinned and revealed her other hand. A round UN logo on a square white backing.

Stone scooped up two handfuls of sticks. [Help me get these back in.] He dumped the sticks into the box. Plastic clattered on plastic, thunderous in the dim silence. Caitlyn kneeled on her skirt and cupped her hands around more sticks—

Noise at the front door. Stone's hand shot to her wrists. He gave her a warning look, then turned to the opaque wall.

The frosted glass muffled a squeaky voice. "If someone wants to put something in the outbound pouch, your office should be open, right?"

"The alarm did not come from here," said Gautam. "It came from the workroom."

Stone tightened his grip on Caitlyn's wrists. [Looks like we tripped an alarm. No problem. Mail clerk called in tower security.]

[No problem!?]

[I invoked Eleven-J on them. I'll talk us out of this.] He stood and faced the door with open palms. She released the sticks from her hands to the beige carpet and mirrored Stone's pose.

The door from the waiting room swung open. The short and muscular security officer burst in. His partner followed. Gray eyes darted around the room, frowned at Caitlyn, then landed on Stone. "All clear."

Gautam's voice came from behind the opaque glass. "That cannot be. I test the alarms every day. It is not possible for there to be a false alarm." Black hair appeared behind the short and muscular officer. Gautam pushed the officer's shoulder and the officer chose to move out of his way.

Gautam stepped through the motion sensor beam. He regarded Stone and Caitlyn and rage boiled in his dark eyes. "Two criminals have broken into the communications office—broken the seal on a diplomatic pouch—and you issue an all clear?"

"They're here on vital UN business," the gray-eyed security officer said.

"How do you know this?"

"I'm not at liberty to say."

Gautam puffed himself up, a Third World bureaucrat asserting authority, either to make a threat or ask for a bribe. Or both. "*I am here on vital UN business.*"

The short and muscular guard spoke in his squeaky voice, "Mr. Lavallette, ma'am, whatever your business, wrap it up soon so we can all forget about this—"

"I said vital UN business." For a moment, Stone didn't recognize the communication clerk's voice. He'd flattened it, given it a tone of dry menace.

Gautam went on. "I invoke Protocol Eleven-J."

Caitlyn sucked in a breath. The security officers shot nervous looks from Stone to Gautam and back.

"Here is the confirmation code," Gautam said. A moment later, the gray-eyed security officer pressed his lips together.

Caitlyn's face regained its usual poise. With a glint in her hazel eyes, she said, "And for the record, here's mine."

The security officer nodded, face pale. Sweat beaded on the short, muscular guard's forehead.

Stone kept his face calm. His mind raced behind it. Who could have Eleven-J clearance other than Caitlyn or him?

Gray's comment on that last spring morning in UNICA headquarters came back. The team to establish the UNICA field office on Minerva traveled under cover on *Yassir Arafat*.

This officious, forgettable Indian was Gray's man on Minerva.... A grin bared Stone's teeth. An excellent cover—

The grin froze. If Gautam checked the manifest of the diplomatic pouch, he'd realize that Stone had stolen the real message to Gray. Then he'd report Stone's action to the old man. Then....

Stone's heart pounded like a gong, loud yet slow. He could still come clean. Enlist Gautam's help to kill Caitlyn and reveal the plot to Gray.

Except Caitlyn's embedded quantum computer would betray him to Bale and the others even after her death. Five soldiers had sneaked up on him before. Even in the tower, could he and Gautam and the encrypted stick all survive to alert Gray?

No. [He's UNICA field office,] Stone said. [We have to kill him.]

[Agreed,] Caitlyn replied.

"Gentlemen," Stone said to the security officers, "this is above your pay grade. You should wait in the hall."

The gray-eyed security officer tapped his partner's shoulder. "Good idea." Both men slipped out. The short, muscular one pulled closed the frosted glass door. The front door to the communications office shut with a click sounding around the edges of the opaque door and window.

"Who the hell are you?" Gautam asked.

"She's ITB. As for me… you and I have a mutual employer."

"What? I'm a communication clerk."

"With Eleven-J authority? Don't blow smoke up my ass and tell me it's a nicotine enema. You're head of the UNICA field office."

Gautam rocked back on his heels. "You're an operative? Which one? Phantom? Hybrid? Sharpshooter?"

"That's not important."

"Yes it is," Gautam said. "I have to include it in my report." His brown-eyed gaze dipped to the heap of memory sticks near the opened box. "Along with why you compromised a diplomatic pouch."

"Gray had evidence that someone with inside knowledge was bringing schematics for the exotic matter factory at Hawking Station to Minerva on *Yassir Arafat*. We're pulling the report he wanted to send to co-conspirators on Earth." A good story to come up with in a few seconds.

Gautam considered. "That would explain her presence. But yours?"

"We're on a joint task force. Someone from ITB to identify the evidence. And a UNICA operative to do good tradecraft."

Through their embedded quantum computer interface, Caitlyn sent Stone an image of her sticking out her tongue.

Gautam sounded like he believed the story. "Where is the pulled report?"

Stone kneeled. Shrugged the toolkit off his shoulder. "In here." The toolkit thumped on the flimsy carpet. Stone reached in.

Gautam leaned forward.

Plastic and stamped steel touched Stone's fingers. He slid the safety off. One smooth motion brought the pistol out, sights to his eye, finger squeezing with extra pressure the heavy trigger.

The pistol roared and kicked against Stone's hand. The tang of propellant filled the air.

Gautam toppled backward. Blood oozed out of a pit in his face where his eye had been. The air stank of blood and brain. Crimson soaked the thin beige carpet.

His body trembled under the last commands of his mangled brain. You have to hit the brain stem to kill a man instantly.

Poor bastard. Doing his job.

Just like I'm doing mine.

Slender fingers touched Stone's shoulder. He got to his feet. Caitlyn kept her mouth shut. Speaking wouldn't work, her ears must ring as loudly as his. [What's our story for the security officers?]

[Nothing.]

[They heard the gunshot!]

Stone's gaze dropped to Gau—the comm clerk's ruined face, then shied away.

What's wrong with you? He's not the first man you've killed.

> *[Stone Chalmers has killed 204 people, of whom 191 were adult males—]*

He swatted the reminder away. The embedded quantum computer shoved facts at him like a hypnogogued cover story? Dammit.

[Adjusting settings.]

[Hey.] Caitlyn's hazel eyes studied him. [Answer my question!]

Her question—

[How can we tell the two men in the hallway that nothing happened?]

[We don't have to. We invoked Protocol Eleven-J. Follow me.]

They carefully went around the dead man's pooling blood. Stone grabbed his toolkit like a wino clutching a bottle in a paper bag. His foot disturbed the heap of memory sticks around the open box. Stone led Caitlyn through the opaque glass door without deactivating the alarms.

In the hallway outside the waiting room, the security officers looked up from a tight huddle. "What happened?" asked the gray-eyed one.

"I can't tell you. For your own protection." Stone reached into the toolkit. "Thanks for loaning me your sidearm." He handed the 9mm to the gray-eyed security officer. "And you can do the UN a great favor. Go to your office, scrub all audio and video from the entire building for the last hour, and leave the cameras and microphones off until we contact you. All should be clear by 2200."

The gray-eyed security officer slipped his pistol into a pocket of his tactical pants. His lips mashed together like he wanted to spit out a mouthful of foul options. "We can do that."

Stone clapped his hand on the security officer's shoulder. In his own ears, his voice sounded brittle. "You two are a credit to the UN. I only wish I could write a commendation."

"Doing a good job is all the commendation we need."

"That's right," echoed the short, muscular one.

"Words to live by," said Stone. He gave the security officer's shoulder an extra squeeze. The man took the hint. The two security officers shuffled down the hall and around the corner to the elevator lobby.

[Now we have to clean up a crime scene in eight hours,] Stone said.

[I'll ask for help.]

[Wait. You're going to bring your Minervan friends into the tower?]

[UN employees are inviting their local contacts to the party. But we don't need my colleagues. Just some items that can help us. Carpet cleaners. Deodorizers. Large scan-proof bags. One of Bradley dell'Angelo's heavy cargo drones.]

[Okay. Go make arrangements. I'll stay here.]

An eyebrow arched over a hazel eye. [Why?]

[I missed a sensor in the workroom. And if that's the UNICA field office, there are recording devices in there too.] Dumping the corpse twenty miles out to sea wouldn't help if Gray found out Stone had killed his field officer.

[Take care of them. I'll contact my friends when I get in the elevator.] Caitlyn set off down the hallway. The slap of her sandals against the carpeted hallway sounded carefree.

Stone went back into the waiting room. He left the outer door unlocked. On the slim chance someone came with a dropoff for the diplomatic pouch, they would expect to enter the waiting room. But when the mail clerk failed to answer at the window, and they tested the locks on the frosted glass door—

He opened the workroom door. The stink of blood and brain hit his nose. Stone slipped in. The door thumped closed. A thumbpress locked the handle; a turn, the deadbolt.

The stench assaulted him more strongly. Stone ignored it as best he could. Secure now, he pulled the scanner from his toolkit. Perhaps they'd stepped on a pressure sensor under the carpet. With his back to the dead man, Stone scanned the carpet along the path they'd taken.

The scanner beeped as soon as he started, where their first steps over the motion sensor beam had landed. Clever placement.

Now to find the recording devices hidden in the room, and the computer saving those devices to memory. He worked methodically, passing the scanner over a foot-wide swathe of the walls, starting next to the ceiling near the door.

He paused with his sleeve brushing the window blind. First pass clear. One foot lower, back toward—

A handle clanked. Hinges sounded. Light from the hallway entered the waiting room and blurred when it hit the frosted glass window.

Stone lowered his arms. He rested the scanner on the floor near his feet, then stood immobile.

A pad of footsteps. The handle to the frosted glass door rattled.

[Caitlyn, is that you?]

[I'm two miles across town.]

[Then who's in the waiting room?]

The deadbolt shot back into the door. A key scraped the tumblers in the handle lock.

The handle turned. "Gautam, you here?"

The door opened. A shock of purple hair. Eyes as white as full moons fixated on Gautam's corpse, then regarded Stone.

CHAPTER 20

Four strides across the room. At his third, Merrill reacted. She shuffled back and pulled the door toward her.

Far too late. Stone's left hand clamped the door. His right hand shot to her neck. Lifted her. Squeezed.

Her eyes seemed even larger now. Gurgles came from her throat. She swung her fists sideways at his face, kicked black canvas sneakers at his shins. His longer reach held her at bay.

He pivoted. The door fell shut. Still strangling her, he shoved her against the shelves. The box of security stickers tumbled to the floor, unrolling a dozen copies of the UN logo. He jammed his left hand past her frantic fists. Plowed his fingers through her hair. His fingernails scraped her scalp, pulled hair, drew blood.

A growing mass of minuscule wires lodged under his nails.

She grabbed his right arm, tried pulling it away from her throat. He squeezed harder. Her face turned blue. Sweat matted her hair to her forehead and stank of her panic.

He kept scraping the transcranial stim wiring from her scalp. It looked like black thread, finer than the purple-dyed hair and blacker than the red droplets of blood coming with it. Had to get enough to block her from making an emergency call.

Her blue face turned purple. Her eyes bulged. She scratched her nails on his arm, acceding to his strength, trying to break his grip with pain. Soaked with adrenaline, he felt only the pressure of her fingers, no pain.

She kicked like a trapped rabbit. Her foot slammed the inside of his right knee.

His leg wobbled. He grunted. Despite his adrenaline pain throbbed.

He grunted and squeezed harder.

The muscles of her throat worked but no sound came. Her eyes rolled back. Her arms fell to her sides.

Stone lowered her feet to the floor, but his grip remained strong. Unconsciousness comes quickly, but her heart had to stop for strangulation to kill.

He looked away, then forced himself to look at her purple, eye-bulged face. A viscous black liquid seemed to run down his spine. He kept looking.

He'd killed women before, even women he'd previously bedded. Granted, those had all been like Teresa Benavides, subjects of his investigation who'd ended up in the UN's crosshairs. Part of the game.

Not like this. Merrill had been doing her job, in a sense. She'd come looking for her boyfriend. The fool had given her a key to a UNICA field office. He'd brought this on her—

Don't. Sure, lie to other people. But don't lie to yourself. You're the one killing her. Yes, you have a good reason. Kill a witness to a crime you committed while committing another crime….

You have a reason, at least. If she lives long enough to get a message to Gray, you die. Either at Gray's hand or those of Caitlyn's Minervan friends. Now, you live one more day.

There was never more than that to his life.

His right arm ached. He checked her pulse with his left. Nothing.

His knee almost buckled under when he moved. He laid Merrill's limp body on the carpet near Gautam's corpse, outside of the crimson splotch of blood-soaked carpet. He checked her wrist, her neck, her chest. No pulse, no breath. Dead.

Stone rocked back with his backside on the floor. Three messages from Caitlyn waited for him. He skipped them, went straight to a call.

She answered in a moment. [What happened?]

[Bring a second body bag,] he said. He expected to hear black humor in his voice yet heard none.

A forest green sedan from the motor pool crouched with its headlights off near the guardrail of the scenic overlook off the coast highway. A hundred yards down the sheer crater wall, the Wisdom Sea crashed waves. Euler City glowed over the horizon, washing out the lowest tiers of northern stars.

Stone limped back from one of the two heavyweight drones. He'd shoved Gautam's stiffening body into the drone's cargo bay despite his swollen, unbendable knee. Caitlyn had offered to let him handle the lighter of the two corpses. He'd declined. Hopefully she accepted it as a gesture of manliness, and didn't see the chasm opening inside him at the thought of handling Merrill's body.

Fool. The same gray blockchain bound them together. She already knew.

"Ready?" she said over the rustle of waves.

"I'm glad Sheila didn't come to facilitate their funerals."

Her face showed as a pale oval against the night. "Me too. She's a good person who knows in her head what we must do. But not in her heart."

The drones' motors hummed. She must have sent the command to them by a thought. The drones rose, unimpeded by their lifeless cargoes, their warning lights turned off. Over the guardrail they flew and headed east over the sea. Night veiled them within seconds.

Five miles out, the drones would open their cargo hatches. The depth and prevailing current would carry the corpses fifty miles further, through habitats of sharks and carrion-eating wolffish. Even if their remains washed ashore in months or years, investigators would write it off as a murder-suicide, strangulation followed by a gunshot to the forehead.

"Sheila's a good person," Stone said. "Unlike us."

Caitlyn stared out to sea. "We do some evil things."

"But the goal justifies them?"

"No. It just makes it easier for me to sleep at night. I didn't think that was a problem for you."

"It's not. It wasn't."

"What do you mean?"

He blew a breath into the chill desert night. "I tell myself I play the greatest game in the settled galaxy. A game where the loser dies. But unless I win every round, I'll end up like them." He looked up in the direction the drones had flown. "Meat to be disposed."

Wind gusted over the crater rim. "You'll end up like them even if you do win every round," Caitlyn said. "You're good at the game. You could be great if you had a reason to play."

He leaned against the sedan and let the pounding waves below set the rhythm of his thoughts.

After a time, a faint buzz over the sea heralded the return of the drones. They emerged from the night and descended over the guardrail. Gently they touched the asphalt. The motors silenced.

Caitlyn reached into the sedan and handed him a spray bottle. He limped over to one of the drones. With one hand, he tilted the drone onto its side rotors. The drone's cargo hatch dangled open. He sprayed a foam of nanomachines on the underside of the hatch and on every surface of the cargo compartment. Caitlyn did the same.

They'd used the same foam in the communication office. For five minutes the foam hissed like a glass of sparkling water. After that, the hissing faded. The foam hardened, then crumbled into powder carried off by the wind.

Caitlyn handed him a can of compressed air. He chased stubborn flecks of the powder from the hatch hinge and corners of the compartment with sharp puffs. One puff jetted bitter grit into his mouth. He winced and spewed breath between tight lips.

"Final check," Caitlyn said.

"I can do this."

"You've done enough. Rest your knee." He limped back to the sedan. A scanner display threw a sickly green light over her as she ran the scanner's wand over the hatch and interiors of both drone cargo compartments. "Clean."

"Send them home," Stone said, but their motors had already spun up. Seconds later they climbed into the sky, heading north toward Bradley dell'Angelo's shoreline facility. Their silhouettes showed briefly against the glow of Euler City before vanishing into the night.

"Our turn," Caitlyn said. The forest green sedan opened its near-side doors. "We should be back fifteen or twenty minutes before the security officers restart the cameras." She stooped to enter, then halted.

"I need to say something," said Stone.

She straightened her back. "Go."

He swallowed. "Earlier, when I agreed to join you, I didn't mean it."

"I know."

"I mean it now."

The night was too dim to make out her agate eyes. "I know that too."

CHAPTER 21

A thunderstorm threw rain like pebbles at Gray's windows. Inside, warm lights, plush chairs, and the peaty aroma of whisky formed a bubble of comfort.

Stone drank sparkling water. Tart juice from a lime wedge mingled with the bitter edge of minerals as he prepared to lie.

Gray angled his head toward one of the monitors on the standing desk behind him to his right. "Minerva isn't the threat I feared."

"I realized that even before the wormhole placement. High technology combined with complete innocence. We'll roll the Minervans before they know what hit them."

"How did you acquire such detailed intelligence on the Center for Alignment with the Universe?"

Stone shrugged with a smirk. "Minerva's ruling class is like any other. They insist on a strict moral code, while underneath they're corrupt as hell."

"You refer in particular to Facilitatrix van Bentum? A woman three times your age?"

Stone's smirk widened. "The things I do for the United Nations."

"Spare me the details." He sipped whisky. "You failed to see a live consecration. Convocation?"

"Consecration is the psych testing they inflict on thirteen-year-olds. Myers-Briggs, enneagram, something like that. Convocation is a form of verbal hazing, like the lemon sessions sorority girls use to make each other conform, or what Third World dictators call struggle sessions, where the capitalists or the communists or whoever publicly admit their crimes. Standard cult stuff."

"So it sounds." Gray picked up his whisky glass. With the shimmering brown liquid near his mouth, he said, "Setting aside your report, what do you know about the double disappearance?"

"The—? Oh, the mail clerk and the girl? People were whispering about it my last three days on Minerva."

"What do you think happened?"

Stone sipped. "The day of the party, the UN staffers were giddy after the successful wormhole placement. By late night, they were hammered drunk as well."

"You observed your father often enough in his last years to know 'hammered drunk' when you see it."

Who the hell was Gray to bring that up? Stone kept the thought off his face. "Anyway, I'd guess they went up on the tower's roof and fell off."

"Both of them?"

"Drunk and giddy? Sure. Why do you care?"

Gray's eyes reminded him of shotgun barrels. "The tower's security systems happened to fail near the start of the party and only resumed working at midnight."

"Hmm. I never heard that." He gazed past Gray at the painting of a sailboat race and looked thoughtful. "No surprise. Those security officers struck me as inept from the day *Yassir Arafat* left Hawking Station."

Gray sipped, then set his whisky on his cherrywood desktop with a thud. "'Never attribute to malice what can be explained by stupidity?'"

"Exactly." Stone sipped mineral water. Gray would soon hint he should leave. Time to bring up what Caitlyn had instructed him to ask. "I won't take more of your time, but before I go, I want time off."

One eyebrow arched. "How much?"

"A month." Stone read the older man's face. "Is that a problem?"

"It's an unexpected request. At the end of your previous mission, you recoiled at an enforced leave of absence."

"That was for six months," Stone said. "And it wasn't my choice or yours."

"True. But why?"

Stone yawned from the red eye flight from LA and the body clock reset from Minerva's shorter day. "I spent a week pretending to be Edward Lavallette, gathered intel from public sources, and no one tried to kill me. It was easier work. I could get used to it. I want to think about it. Make sure before I request reassignment."

Gray blinked once, then nudged at the knot in his necktie. "There are times you surprise me, Hybrid. You have your month. Use it well."

"Thanks." Stone threw the rest of his sparkling water down his throat, then rose from the plush chair.

"Wait."

Stone stood, left hand like a crane holding the empty glass. "Yes?"

"I only learned after your return that Caitlyn Fredriksen had journeyed to Minerva with the diplomatic mission and stayed until after the wormhole placement. Did you know that?"

"No." Stone shrugged.

"Would you have sought her out if you had known?"

"Sought? You mean ask her out on a date?" Stone laughed. "No. Never. My relationship with her is purely business."

ABOUT THE AUTHOR

I'M **RAYMUND EICH.** I use my Middle American upbringing as a launchpad for journeys to the ends of the Universe.

Growing up in the Midwest prepared me for my academic career, culminating with a Ph.D. in biochemistry from Rice University. It helps me help inventors prosper from their progress in medicine, biotechnology, and green energy.

Above all, it inspires me to write science fiction and fantasy about ordinary people facing extraordinary wonders and horrors, battling enemies both foreign and domestic, and building better lives for themselves, their families, and their societies.

My last name has one syllable and is pronounced "eye-sh." I live in Houston with my family.

Connect with me at **www.raymundeich.com** or follow the QR code below.

Online and brick-and-mortar bookstores around the world list millions of books, with thousands more published every day. I'm glad you discovered this one.

If you'd like to know when I release a new book, instead of leaving it to chance, join my Readers Club. I'll email you from time to time with publishing news, off-beat patents, a short personal update, or a reminder about an older book of mine you might have missed.

Yes, please! I'll go to **www.raymundeich.com/mailing-list** or scan the QR code below.

No thanks. I'll take my chances next time I look for your books.

OTHER BOOKS BY THE AUTHOR

Available wherever books are sold.

Learn more about these titles at our website, **www.cv2books.com,** or follow the QR code below.

STONE CHALMERS

Earth barely survived the 21st Century.

Biotechnological and nuclear terrorism, civil war, famine, and ethnic cleansing killed billions. Thousands fled on warpdrive ships to colonize planets around distant suns.

In the 22nd century, after Earth unified under one world government, it opened wormhole links to the distant colonies, to prevent a repeat of the previous century's chaos on a galactic scale.

Enter operative Stone Chalmers. Spy. Assassin. Instrument maintaining Earth's dominion over all human worlds.

Opposing him are hostile forces on colony worlds… and within the Earth government itself.

When Stone clashes with those forces, Earth—and every human world—will be transformed forever.

Learn more about the Stone Chalmers series at **www.cv2books.com/stone-chalmers**, or follow the QR code below.

The Freeland Vendetta

On the newly rediscovered colony world Freeland, a conspiracy plans a powerful blow against Earth's control of the planet. A blow supported by treacherous forces inside the government of Earth.

The Trinity Deception

From the religious colony world of Trinity come clues of a long-lost prize. The last warpdrive ship outside Earth's control.

The Minerva Conspiracy

Expecting a mission beneath his talents, Stone fights for his life—and soul—against a terrifying conspiracy.

The Terra Betrayal

Schemes and plots from the colonies and the capital converge in the halls of power on Earth itself. Only Stone can fight his way through a web of intrigue and bring freedom to all human worlds.

THE INCEPTI CATACLYSM

The entire galaxy knows about the Incepti Cataclysm. The occupation force from Vela destroyed a planet with nanotechnology. Only a few Inceptis fled the wave of death in time to join their brethren scattered across the Democracy.

Everything the galaxy knows is a lie.

Anara Orden. Daughter of survivors. Recruited by fellow Inceptis to join Democracy intelligence. Though young and good of heart, she kills without qualms. She knows her employers only order her to terminate Velan agents threatening the Democracy.

But when her next target is a fellow Incepti, she questions everything and chooses a new mission. She will share the truth with friend and foe alike.

Yet powerful forces across the galaxy will do whatever it takes to cling to power. Even if millions of innocents must die.

Escape from Conatus (Book One)

When Anara learns the truth, a simple mission becomes a flight for survival.

Revelation in Vela (Book Two)

Instead of a refuge, Anara and her companions end up in the cross-hairs—of two sides.

Victory for Carina (Book Three)

As war comes to the galaxy, only Anara's desperate plan can bring a just and lasting peace.

THE FALSE FLAG WAR

Concordia's mission reflected the best of the human race. Crew and scientists from both of Earth's rival factions, Humanists and Traditionalists, journeyed for years at relativistic speeds to reach Bravo Charlie, a life-bearing planet orbiting Alpha Centauri B, to expand the frontiers of knowledge for all.

Concordia's mission also reflected humanity at its worst. Corrupt bureaucrats and ambitious political leaders in both factions maintained a status quo backed by weapons of mass destruction. The faction commanders on the mission each sought to seize advantages for their side alone.

Then the ship received transmissions. Signs of an ancient, powerful alien presence on the planet below.

Exploration 2127

Sent to explore, **Jaeger** and **McIlroy**, born and raised in a Texas divided by razor wire and minefields. Men torn between the mission's ideals and orders from their respective faction commanders, oily Varanathan and domineering Sandford.

Then Jaeger and McIlroy discover how to bring Earth's factions together... using knowledge given by aliens dead over a million years.

Invasion 2132

Concordia fell silent. Mission control now detects an unknown ship leaving the Alpha Centauri system. Heading to Earth at relativistic speeds. Silent about its purpose. Its crew unknown.

Earth's one chance: Its rival factions must work for mutual defense, against shadowy figures who strive to use the unknown ship for their own faction's gain.

THE CONFEDERATED WORLDS

The purpose of all other combat arms is to put the infantryman in sole possession of the battlefield.

A thousand years from now, while Earth sleeps in virtual reality, three polities —the Confederated Worlds, the Unity, and the Progressive Republic—strive to connect the scattered, terraformed worlds of humankind by artificial wormholes.

When they meet, they clash, in a decades-long struggle of arms that will embroil every human world, in which dedication to duty liberates worlds— and oneself.

Learn more about the Confederated Worlds series at **www.cv2books.com/the-confederated-worlds**, or follow the QR code below.

Take the Shilling

The Confederated Worlds implanted in his brain the skills to make him a soldier. Tomas Neumann had to learn for himself how to survive interstellar war.

Operation Iago

The Confederated Worlds lost the war. Can Lt. Tomas Neumann win the peace against elusive, deceptive foes out to turn the Confederated Worlds against itself?

A Bodyguard of Lies

Assigned to the halls of power, only Capt. Tomas Neumann can save the Confederated Worlds from the ultimate treachery.

OTHER NOVELS

The Blank Slate

Neuroscience entrepreneur Clay Shieffer must stop a tyrannical president… because he unwittingly gave the tyrant power over the human mind.

New California

After New California's founder committed suicide, two men vied to rule the colony.

Ashwin George, supported by the colony's elite and the Chinese company dominating half the settled galaxy.

Against him, Desmond Park, nanotechnology engineer, armed with the most formidable weapon of all.

A single idea.

The Reincarnation Run

Skeptical spacejock Landry Krieger knows exactly how to smuggle the "reborn" spiritual leader of an oppressed people past their conquerors… but the boy's priests—and governess—shake up his orderly plans.

Azureseas: Cantrell's War

Ross Cantrell joined the animal control mission on the newly-discovered planet Azureseas to earn the money to start married life together with his girlfriend.

Then Ross discovers the truth about the planet's "animals."

SHORT NOVELS

Love and Death in the City of Bone

He had a month to learn the planet's mysteries—and Juliette's.

His cover story: return to Elard to dismantle his sect's missionary work to the planet's natives.

His true mission: investigate decades-old mysteries of love and death.

His objective: return to Earth with his discovery.

If he can.

A Mighty Fortress

Theodore and his team from the Lutheran Interstellar Terraforming Society would transform a barren, rocky world into a refuge of faith and life.

Or die trying.

Winner and the Poacher

A Portia Oakeshott, Dinosaur Veterinarian Short Novel

As a consultant to law enforcement, Portia confronts stark evidence of a rich young man's crime: the mounted head of a massive herbivorous *Wintonotitan*. A winner.

A dinosaur the company never granted a permit for hunting.

These wonders and more await in the fourth volume of the Complete Science Fiction Stories of Raymund Eich.